Also by Sarah Prineas

The Magic Thief
The Magic Thief: Lost
The Magic Thief: Found
Winterling

Sarah Prineas

SUMMERKIN

HARPER
An Imprint of HarperCollins*Publishers*

Library of Congress Cataloging-in-Publication Data
Prineas, Sarah.
    Summerkin / Sarah Prineas. — First edition.
       pages cm
    Sequel to: Winterling.
    Summary: After defeating the evil Mór, Fer must compete in a
contest that will either seal her fate as the ruler of the Summerlands
or send her back to the human world forever.
    ISBN 978-0-06-192106-3 (hardcover bdg.) [1. Magic—Fiction.
2. Identity—Fiction. 3. Shapeshifting—Fiction. 4. Contests—Fiction.
5. Fantasy.] I. Title.
PZ7.P93646Su 2013   2012026751
[Fic]—dc23   CIP
                                                          AC

Typography by Andrea Vandergrift
13 14 15 16 17   LP/RRDH   10 9 8 7 6 5 4 3 2 1
❖
First Edition

To Greg van Eekhout.
All the bunnies in this book,
both alive and dead, are for you.

prologue

Stupid messenger.

Stupid, stupid messenger who should have known better than to accept a ride from a black horse with a wild mane and flame-bright yellow eyes. The horse galloped up and down hills, through a cold river and a patch of brambles, ending at a swamp, where he bucked the messenger off.

The horse shook his head and spat something from his mouth, and the air around him blurred and a boy with black hair and yellow eyes caught the shifter-bone he'd spat out and shoved it into the pocket of his ragged shorts. Picking his way through the mud and cattails, the boy crouched at the side of the messenger.

"Cursed puck," the messenger groaned, and struggled

onto his knees. He was tall and willowy and had greeny-blond hair, rough brown skin, and long fingers. He'd been sent from the nathe, the court of the High Ones.

"Just stay down," the boy said, and shoved him back into the mud. Then he reached into the messenger's leather pouch and pulled out a letter. The paper was only a little damp at the edges. Cracking the wax seal that held the letter closed, he read it.

Hmm. A message for Lady Gwynnefar. Fer, that was.

The boy got to his feet and trudged out of the muddy swamp to dry land, where he paused to think about what he was going to do. He could throw the letter away. That'd cause some trouble. Or he could give it back to the messenger to deliver. What he should do was give it to his brother pucks to see what they would make of it. More trouble, to be sure. Or . . .

Or he could take the letter and its trouble to the Lady Gwynnefar himself.

one

The girl named Fer pulled back the string of her bow, sighted down the arrow, and released it.

Thunk.

Not quite a bullseye, but almost. Fer shrugged her shoulders, feeling the tiredness in her muscles from an hour of archery practice. Time to stop. It was getting too dark, anyway, and Grand-Jane would have dinner ready soon.

After collecting her arrows from the target—and the one arrow that had gone past the target and was stuck in a clump of weeds—Fer went to sit on the back steps of her grandma's house, and gazed up at the half-moon. The sky was the deep blue, electric color that meant the sun was gone and night was coming soon. As she watched the moon, Fer felt like she could practically see it walking across the sky as time rushed past.

In the Summerlands, on the other side of the Way and far from this human world, time passed much more slowly. There, spring was just ending. The forests would be bursting with new leaves, wildflowers, ferns, and mushrooms; the moss would be cool and dark underfoot.

A creak from the kitchen door, and Fer's grandma came down the steps. She wore a cardigan against the chill of the early autumn night. Grand-Jane came to sit beside her. Fer leaned, and Grand-Jane put her arm around Fer's shoulders. They sat in silence for a while.

Then, "I know," Grand-Jane said.

Fer blinked. "You know what?"

"You're thinking about the other land."

Fer nodded. She was the Lady of the land on the other side of the Way—the Summerlands—and even though she wasn't entirely sure, yet, what being a Lady meant, she did know that she was supposed to be there, not here in the human world. "I have to go back," she said quietly.

Grand-Jane sighed. In the moonlight, her graying hair shone, making her look like a queen with a silver crown. "Yes, I know."

"Why don't you come with me?" Fer asked.

Grand-Jane shook her head. "Look at this place, Jennifer."

What? Fer had lived here almost her whole life. There wasn't anything new to see.

When Fer didn't move, Grand-Jane got up from the steps and pulled Fer to her feet, then took her by the shoulders and turned her to look out at the fields beyond the house. The beehives at the edge of the yard glowed white under the moonlight. Past that was the lavender field, which they'd spent the last few days harvesting, cutting the stalks of purple flowers under the rich, late-September sunlight. Past Grand-Jane's land were more farms, rolling out to a flat horizon under a darkening sky.

The land here had once been wild, and not even that long ago. Just over a hundred years before, it had been prairies full of wildflowers and grasses and buzzing insects, with patches of oak woodlands, and streams winding their way to the river. Lightning-lit wildfires would race through the dry prairie, leaving it blackened, and in the spring new green would sprout up.

Now this land was all tame. It had been shaped into farms that were like giant factories for growing corn and soybeans, acres and acres of fields laid out in careful squares and rectangles. The rich dirt was stained with insecticide and herbicide and chemical fertilizers. Just the smell of it made Fer feel itchy.

How could Grand-Jane want to live *here*?

"This is my home," Grand-Jane said. "This is where I belong."

Fer shrugged out of her grandmother's grip. "Well, it's not where I belong."

"I *know*," Grand-Jane said for the third time. In the rules of the Summerlands, saying something three times made it matter. Grand-Jane knew this, and it meant she understood; she really did know how Fer felt. She added quietly, "I won't try to keep you here, my girl."

"Thank you." Fer breathed. She leaned in, and Grand-Jane gave her a hug. Under her feet, she felt the earth turning and the time flowing away, and suddenly, like a sharp tugging at her heart, she knew that she'd been away from the Summerlands for too long. She had to go back.

She had to go *now*.

Crouching, Fer rested her fingertips on the cool, smooth surface of the moon-pool that connected the human world to the other land. She felt the tingle of the Way opening, and the half-moon reflected in the water changed, rippling into a nearly full moon.

Fer stood up and took one last look around the darkening clearing, at the flowerless laurel bushes, the moss, the tangled branches. Grand-Jane hadn't been happy about her leaving so suddenly. "At least wait until morning," she had protested. But Fer couldn't wait any longer. Taking a deep breath, holding tightly to her bow, she jumped into the pool.

Down through the Way she fell, feeling the wind and the pressing darkness, the dizzy thump when she landed on the bank of the pool on the other side. She kept her eyes closed until her head stopped spinning. When she opened her eyes, she saw that the golden, almost-full moon had moved into the sky, and the half-moon, the moon that belonged in Grand-Jane's world, now lay reflected in the pool. She was through. The air felt softer here, the shadows deeper and more mysterious—and the pull of her connection to the land settled into her bones.

Unlike in the human world, the laurel here was in bloom, the white flowers glowing in the moonlight. A sudden wind sprang up and made the trees around the clearing toss their leafy heads. As Fer climbed to her feet, a tendril of cool breeze wound from her legs to the top of her head, making goose bumps pop up on her arms. She rubbed them down and looked around the dim clearing and into the dark shadows of the forest. Was somebody here? She gripped her bow tightly and got ready to pull an arrow from the quiver on her back. Another breeze wafted past, bringing with it the smell of dirt and fallen leaves.

The branches around the moon-pool rustled. She

strained her eyes, trying to peer into the darkness. Suddenly she felt her connection to the land—the Summerlands—more strongly than ever before. It felt like a surge of green sweeping up from her feet to the top of her head, as if the forest itself was on the move, a stirring in the roots. Then all fell quiet, the clearing filling up like a cup with stillness. Fer held her breath, listening. She heard nothing but a humming silence. She blinked. Shadows crowded in. The clearing had been empty, and now she was surrounded by—

What *were* they?

Standing in a circle around the moon-pool were creatures that looked part tree and part stump, gnarled and covered with lichen and moss. Some of them were shorter than she was; others towered overhead like the tallest trees. In the dim light, Fer saw wise old faces watching her from eyes that glimmered like stars reflected in deep water.

These creatures—whatever they were—had roots that went very, very deep. They were more part of the land than anything she'd ever felt before. And they'd been waiting for her to return.

"Who are you?" she whispered.

The answer came on a breath of wind that brushed past her ears, making her shiver. *We are the deep-forest kin. We have come to swear our oaths to the Lady of the*

Summerlands. Will you accept our oaths?

She hadn't had enough time to think about this. She was the Lady, yes. She knew that because of her bone-deep connection to this land and its people, and because her mother had been the Lady before, until the Mór had killed her.

But the swearing of oaths? That was tricky. Oaths were—well, they were part of how these other lands worked. *Our oaths and our rules bind us together*, the Mór had told her once. The Mór had been evil, through and through, but she'd been right about that. Yet oaths felt wrong, too. The Mór had used oaths to bind her people so strongly that she had controlled their every move. Fer wasn't sure about how to be a Lady, but she did know that she didn't want to bind her people like that.

Will you accept our oaths? the deep-forest ones asked again.

"I—I don't like oaths," Fer said, stalling.

There was a swaying of branches and a rush of wind that sounded like whispers. *It is the way of the land that we should be bound to the Lady*, they breathed.

Fer shook her head. Her best friend, Rook, had been bound to the Mór by his sworn oaths, and it had meant he'd had no choice but to obey her every order. He'd been forced to do things that he'd hated doing. This just couldn't be right.

Will you accept our oaths? they asked a third time. Three had power. She had to answer.

"No," Fer said slowly. "I'm really sorry. I can't."

Her words hung in the air. *Can't—can't—can't*. The deep-forest kin gazed at her, and Fer could feel the weight of their disappointment, as if she'd failed a test.

The deep green feeling faded, and so did the heavy moss and dirt smell in the air. When she looked up again, the clearing around the moon-pool was empty.

two

The Lady Tree was where the Lady of the Summerlands lived, an immensely tall beech with a straight trunk covered in silvery-smooth bark. At the base of the tree, the trunk was so wide that six badger-men could hold hands around it and still not span its girth. It was so tall that it towered over the rest of the forest. Overhead were spreading branches tipped with leaves, turning the light a dappled green. In the lower branches perched the wood-shingled tree house where Fer lived, and other houses, and ladders hanging from branches down to the ground, and swaying rope bridges leading from one platform to another. A whole tree village.

If she closed her eyes, Fer could feel a faint thread of connection to every one of the people who lived in that tree village and in the rest of the Summerlands, a thread just like the connection she felt to the land itself. It was her belonging; it meant she was home.

As Fer stepped out of the forest, one of her wolf-guards came bounding over the grass toward her. It was Fray—brown-haired, sharp-toothed, and rangy tall. All of the people of the Summerlands were people, but they had a wild part—a tree part, or a flower part, or an animal part. Fray was a person, but she had a little bit of wolf in her too, and it made her fierce and brave and loyal, perfect for guarding and fighting. Fray was only a little bit older than Fer, but she wasn't a friend. She was way too serious about her duties for that.

"Lady Gwynnefar!" Fray panted, coming to stand before Fer. She bowed. "You've returned!"

Fer felt a smile bubbling up, and she grinned at Fray. "I have!" It was so, so good to be home. But then the weight of the deep-forest kin's disappointment settled onto her shoulders. "Fray, I saw the deep-forest kin."

Fray's eyes widened. "They came all this way to swear their oaths to the new Lady, didn't they?"

Fer nodded and pulled her long braid around to tug at the end, nervous. "I didn't let them." She held her breath, waiting for Fray's reaction. Had she done the right thing?

Fray stared. "They asked to swear their oaths and you said no?"

Fer's heart sank. "That's right. I said no."

"But Lady," Fray protested. "You must take their oaths—and ours, too."

"Fray," Fer said, frustrated, "it doesn't make any sense. When you had to swear oaths to the Mór, it was a terrible thing." Really terrible. All of the people in the Summerlands had been slaves to the Mór, bound by their oaths to serve her, even though she was evil. "Why do you want to be bound like that again? It's *wrong*."

"No," Fray said stubbornly. "It's right. We need oaths to keep us together."

Fer shook her head. "But I feel connected to all of you!"

"No," Fray repeated. "It's supposed to be the other way."

"What way?" Fer asked.

Fray stared mutely at her, as if Fer was just supposed to *know*.

And maybe a true Lady *would* know.

Frustrated, Fer turned away and headed toward the ladder that led to her tree house. Fray trotted after her. At the tree, Fer started up the ladder, then paused, looking down. Fray looked up beseechingly at her, and Fer felt the wolf-girl's confusion. "I'm sorry," she said, shaking her head. "I just can't take oaths the way the Mór did."

She hurried up the ladder, Fray following. As Fer reached her house on its platform, a swarm of fat golden bees swirled out the door and buzzed loudly around her head. Startled, Fer flinched away from them and felt Fray's strong hand at her back, keeping her from falling right off the platform. A bee zipped past her nose; another one bumbled into her ear, buzzing loudly. Fer gasped a very unladylike *"Eep!"*

"It's all right," Fray said. "They're the Lady's bees."

Fer brushed a bee away from her face. "Mine?"

"They were your mother's bees," Fray explained. "The Lady Laurelin's. They never came for the Mór, but they're here for you. They can talk, but the only one who can understand them is . . ." She paused and gave Fer a significant glance. ". . . the Lady. You, that means. You see, Lady Gwynnefar?" Fray went on. "The bees showing up like this, it means you're the Lady, and you need to let all your people swear our oaths to you."

That was *not* what it meant. Fer shrugged Fray's hand off her back and ducked inside her house to drop off her bow and quiver full of arrows. Then she headed up the ladder that led from her house platform, climbing higher and higher into the tree where nobody would follow.

When she got to a high branch she swung off the ladder and, balancing carefully, crawled out a little way and lay down. Closing her eyes, feeling the branch solid under her back, she reached out to feel the land. *Her* land. It was mostly forest, the trees like a leafy ocean washing up over hills, pooling in shady valleys. She felt the Lady Tree itself, stretching its graceful branches up to catch the summer sun's rays, pushing its roots ever deeper into the ground. And it was wild, all of it—a wild and untamed land that would never be turned into neat, square cornfields.

She heard the sound of buzzing and opened her eyes. The bees had joined her, swirling lazily over her head. "Hello, bees," she said.

The bees swarmed around her with a sound like drowsy summer afternoons in her grandma's lavender fields. But these weren't honeybees, not like Grand-Jane's bees. In the greeny-gold light of the tree, the Lady's bees looked like plump golden bullets, each with a vicious stinger at its back end. Fer strained to listen, trying to hear words in their humming.

Hmmmmmm-zzzm-zzm-zm went the bees, round and round. Fer closed her eyes. Nothing. She listened harder. A breeze blew and the leaves whispered, but if the bees said anything, Fer couldn't understand what it was.

Hmmmm-zmm-rrrm-zm, the bees grumbled.

From way down below came the faint sound of growling, a shout and a shriek, and then three fierce barks.

Fer's eyes popped open. Did she know a dog who barked like that? A dog who might be down there fighting with the wolf-guards?

The bees spun out of their orbit around her, and Fer let them go, sitting up and peering down. She was so high in the tree that she couldn't see much, just a few of her people moving around, two of them at the edge of a platform looking up at her. The fox-girls—Twig and her sister, Burr—both of them short and thin as saplings, with reddish hair. Fer waved at them, and they waved back, then pointed at the tree's wide trunk. She looked over at the ladder and saw a dark form coming up, the top of a black-haired head. The form became a person, who swung off the ladder and onto the branch above hers.

"Rook!" Fer hadn't seen him since she'd become the Lady back in the early spring.

He crouched and glared down at Fer. "Stupid wolves," he growled.

Rook wore ragged shorts and nothing else; his hair was tangled, and his bare legs were muddy and scratched, as if he'd been running through a bramble patch. He had scars on his arms and shoulder from the wolf bites he'd gotten while serving the Mór. They looked like jagged white slashes against his tan skin.

Without saying hello, Rook lay down on the branch. He glanced at her, and she grinned at him.

"Don't be looking at me like that," he said.

"Like what?" she asked, still smiling.

"I don't know. As if you're glad to see me."

"I *am* glad to see you," Fer said. "You're my best friend."

He stared at her. "No, I'm not. I'm a puck."

Before, when she had first met him, Rook had been oath-bound to the Mór, the false Lady who had ruled this place after she killed Fer's mother—and that meant he'd been like the Mór's slave and had to obey her every order. Rook had sworn those oaths to save his puck-brother Phouka's life. Even so, he had found a way to help Fer defeat the Mór, though he had almost died doing it. With the Mór defeated and gone from the Summerlands, Rook had been freed from his oaths—he was a puck unbound. Grand-Jane had warned Fer that this Rook would be a different creature entirely from the Rook Fer had known before. *Don't trust him*, Grand-Jane had said with a dire frown. *He is a puck, and that means it is his nature to be false, a liar and a trickster. He is not your friend.*

"I missed you," Fer found herself saying. "What have you been up to?"

Rook shrugged.

She shrugged back at him, crossed her eyes, and grinned.

He turned his face away, but she caught a glimpse of a smile.

Fer had heard Grand-Jane's warnings, but she couldn't help the happiness that bubbled up inside her. He could be surly and rude, but that was what made him Rook, and the Rook she knew was a true friend. "Well," she went on. "Why have you come back?"

He looked as if he was weighing a decision. Then he dug in the pocket of his ragged shorts and pulled out a packet of paper. "I met a messenger," he said, "and I offered him a ride in my horse form."

As a puck, Rook had a shifter-tooth that turned him into a black dog when he put it under his tongue, and he had a bit of shifter-bone that turned him into a horse.

"So where is this messenger now?" Fer asked.

"He accepted the ride," Rook said, shooting her an evil grin.

Uh-oh. "What did you do with him, Rook?" she asked sternly.

Rook shrugged. "He's all right. If he can swim. He was bringing you this." He tossed the packet of paper toward her.

Fer reached out to catch it and felt herself slipping. She grabbed the packet out of the air and with her other hand clung to the branch; her head spun, and her stomach lurched, and below her she saw a whirl of branches and leaves and empty space. It was a long way to the ground. When she righted herself, she found Rook was watching her, a gleam of mischief in his flame-bright eyes.

He'd done that on purpose, thrown the paper so she'd reach for it and almost fall. Grand-Jane's warning echoed in her head: *He is not your friend.*

"See?" Rook said. "Puck."

"Puck or not," Fer grumbled to herself, "you're still my friend." With shaking hands, she unfolded the paper and saw that it was a letter that had been sealed with a blob of scented golden wax stamped with a foxglove flower. A good medicinal herb, foxglove, if used properly, but deadly poison in larger doses. A strange choice for a seal. She wondered whose it was. The seal was broken and the paper smudged and wrinkled. "You read this?"

Rook lay back on his branch again and closed his eyes. "So what if I did?"

Fer took a deep breath and didn't answer. She read the letter.

To Gwynnefar of the Summerlands, greetings from the High Ones.

We have received word that you defeated the Mór, who was your mother the Lady Laurelin's betrayer and who stained the land with blood, and that you have cleansed the land of this stain. We have been told, too, that your father was one Owen, a human man.

We are aware that you have the ability to open the Way between the human world and our own lands, and a Lady's glamorie, and that you have a Lady's power to feel the Summerlands and its people. And we hear also that you are a healer of some note.

You would claim to be Lady of the Summerlands, yet you yourself are a human usurper until you have proven yourself worthy to us, the High Ones who rule over all the Lands.

Thus we summon you at once to the nathe, where you may compete with those who would also claim the right to rule the Summerlands. Should you fail to win this competition, you will be cast back into the human world and the Way to our lands closed to you forever.

"Wait," Fer muttered. "They say I have to prove myself?" She read the letter again. It sounded bad. As if the High Ones, whoever they were, didn't believe she was really the Lady, even though the Summerlands sang in her blood, and she felt a spiderweb thread of connection to every one of the people who lived here. "What's the *nathe*?" she asked Rook, not sure if he would answer or not.

Rook hopped from his branch to crouch next to her. "It's the High Ones' court," he answered. "It's where they live."

And the High Ones ruled over all the Lords and Ladies and all the lands on this side of the Way, it sounded like. Fer frowned. If she ignored the letter, she risked losing the Summerlands and its people, and she couldn't bear that, not after all she'd done to free them from the Mór, not when being here felt so *right*. But proving herself in a competition? She shivered. Still . . . "I have to go, don't I?"

"You do, yes," Rook said, his voice quiet, without a trace of mischief in it.

She looked over at him, straight into his eyes. She could easily see the wildness in him, and the darkness. He was a puck, yes. He followed no rules but his own. But that didn't matter. She'd saved his life three times, and he'd risked his life again to help her defeat the Mór. He was the best friend she'd ever had. "Will you come with me?" she asked.

He flinched as if she'd hit him, then shook his head and jumped to his feet. "I won't, no," he snarled, and then stalked off along the branch to the tree trunk, where he swung himself onto the ladder and climbed down.

Fer stared after him. It hadn't been such a terrible thing to ask, had it?

This new Rook was going to take a lot of getting used to.

three

In his dog form, Rook raced away from the Lady Tree, cursing himself. Going to see Fer had been *tame*, and stupid, and he'd really done her a favor, hadn't he, delivering the letter from the High Ones when he should have given it to his brother-pucks to make trouble with. It was a good thing his brothers would never know that he'd had the letter in his hands and had given it away.

Panting, he trotted on, his paws silent and sure on the mossy ground, his black fur blending with the shadows of the late-afternoon forest. Arriving at a clearing at the edge of Fer's land, he spat the shifter-tooth from his mouth and felt the blurring dizziness of the change. He caught the tooth in his hand and shoved it into his pocket. His head down, he went on. No, he wouldn't go back to see Fer again. Fer, with her strange, human ideas about friendship. As if a puck could ever truly be friends with anyone but another puck.

Yes, it'd be better for her if he stayed away.

The sky, what he could see of it through the trees, grew darker, and shadows gathered in the branches overhead. He set off across a clearing gray with twilight.

"Hellooooo, Rook," came a voice from behind him.

He whirled, but nobody was there.

He turned back, and Tatter stood before him, grinning. "Rook!" Tatter exclaimed, and pulled him into a rough hug.

Rook grinned back at his brother-puck. Tatter was older—almost all of the other pucks were older than he was—and taller, and wore his black hair in a matted mane down his back. His skin was the red-brown color of oak leaves in the autumn; for clothes he wore a shapeless wrap made of tattered and stained yellow silk. His flame-orange eyes danced. "Haven't seen you in ages, Rook-pup."

"I've been around," Rook said.

"No you haven't." Tatter gave him a quick cuff on the side of the head. "You've been playing hard-to-find." He looped an arm over Rook's shoulders, then pulled him closer to kiss the spot where he'd hit him. "Come on," he said, bringing Rook along with him. "Asher wants to see you."

In his chest, Rook felt a surge of longing mixed with a curl of fear. Pucks didn't like to be alone; they tended to gather with other pucks, and wherever they gathered, that was their home. Ever since the trouble with the Mór, Rook had been keeping himself apart. He mostly wanted to see Asher and the others, but part of him wanted to run away and hide. Asher was not going to like what he'd gotten himself mixed up in. Still, if Asher called, a puck did well to answer, or his life would get very tricky.

Tatter shifted into his dog form, and Rook did too, and they trotted through the growing night to the nearest Way. Ways that led from one land to another, like doors that led from one room to another, were kept open so that anyone—even pucks—could come and go as they wished. This Way led from the twilit clearing in Fer's Summerlands to another Way that lay at the bottom of a steep hill crowded with brambles, then to the next Way, which waited in the shadow of a huge boulder, to a last Way that led to the Foglands, where a chilly wind whistled through the bare branches over their heads and leaves crunched under their paws. They passed over that land like two dog-shaped shadows until they came to a high cliff. Overhead, a half-moon shone down. Tatter spat out his shifter-tooth, and so did Rook.

The chilly breeze brushed across his bare shoulders, and Rook shivered, missing his black fur, and wishing for more clothes than just his ragged shorts.

"Not far now," Tatter said, and led Rook along the cliff until they reached a path so narrow they had to go up it sideways, clinging to handholds that were bumps of shadow in the harsh moonlight.

Rook felt the cold cliff face grating against his chest and tried not to look down at the dark ground below as they climbed higher. His fingers grew numb from gripping the knobs of rock that kept him from falling off.

"Just here," Tatter said, crouched down, and disappeared.

Rook edged farther along until he saw a deeper shadow in the cliff face. An opening. Stooping, he crawled through, then around a corner, coming out into a cave. It was wide and high ceilinged, with smooth, sand-colored stone walls and a bright fire burning at its center. His eyes automatically searched for another way out, then found it—two openings in a side wall, tunnels, no doubt, that led outside. No puck would let himself be caught in a place without a back exit.

"Look who I brought!" Tatter was announcing, and then, as Rook climbed to his feet, he heard *Brother! Puppy! It's our Rook!* echoing from the cave walls, and a few cheerful yips from the other pucks lounging around the fire. All of them jumped up and gathered around Rook, hugging him and tousling his hair. A younger puck toddled over and grabbed Rook's knees, grinning up at him. He found himself laughing and returning hugs, and buzzing with sudden happiness.

Then another puck pushed through the crowd and seized Rook in a fierce hug. Asher was lithe and tall, had skin tinged ashy gray, and wore gleaming crystals woven into his many long black braids. His eyes burned with a redder flame than most yellow-eyed pucks.

He gripped Rook's shoulders and looked him over, his eyes narrowing when he saw the scars from the wolf bites. "Ah, it's our young Rook, come home at last," Asher said. "How we've missed you!"

He'd missed them, too. Being bound to the Mór, being away from his brother-pucks—it had been like having a hollow, empty place inside him. Seeing them again filled it up, to overflowing.

He bent down and picked up the baby, Scrap, and hugged him. "Hello, little one," he whispered. Rook himself had found the abandoned baby-puck and brought him to his brothers when Scrap had been tiny. As the next-youngest of the pucks, Rook had spent many long nights feeding the baby with stolen milk and rocking him to sleep. "And here you are, walking on your own legs like a grown-up lad," Rook said, giving the baby a kiss. Scrap squirmed and laughed, his yellow eyes alight, and Rook set him on the stone floor. Scrap staggered away, and another puck caught him before he could fall and took him away to the warm fire that blazed at the center of the cave.

"Come on," Asher said. "We want to talk to you." The other pucks faded away, went back to sit by the fire. Asher put an arm around Rook's bare shoulders and pulled him to a darker corner of the cave. Tatter came too.

Another puck was waiting for them, crouched in shadow. Rip, it was, sharp-faced and wearing nothing at all except for swirls of red and black paint on his skin. He gave Rook a narrow-eyed nod.

Rook shivered and nodded back.

"You're cold, Rook-pup," Tatter said, settling on a pile of blankets. "Have a shirt." He dug into a bag at his feet and pulled out a wad of stained green cloth, which he tossed to Rook.

"Thanks," Rook said, and pulled the shirt over his head. It must've come from somebody even bigger than Fer's wolf-guards, because its ragged hem hung almost to his knees and the sleeves were too long.

Asher went to lean against the smooth cave wall,

where he looked Rook up and down. "Been out wandering?"

Rook nodded, then busied himself with rolling up the sleeves of his new shirt.

"From the looks of those scars, you've been fighting." Asher glanced aside at Rip. "Wouldn't you say, Brother?"

"Wolves, at a guess," Rip answered from the shadows.

"Should've asked your brothers for help dealing with them," Asher said, testing.

Rook shrugged. It'd happened too fast to ask for help with the wolves or with anything else. Rook had been on his way to see his puck-brother Finn and had arrived just as the Mór was about to kill him in one of her bloody hunts. The only thing she would take in return for sparing Finn's life was Rook's thrice-sworn oath, and that had bound him to her more tightly than iron chains.

"Didn't you miss us?" Asher went on.

"I did, yes," Rook answered.

"But you didn't ask us for help." Asher's voice had turned cold. "And you were gone such a long time."

"A long time," Rip echoed, his narrow eyes fixed on Rook.

Rook stared at them, not sure what to say. Behind him, the rest of the pucks in the cave, even the baby, had fallen silent, as if they were all listening to hear how

Rook would explain why he'd stayed away from home for so long.

Suddenly Asher grinned. "It's all right, Puppy. We know about your little troubles with the Mór. Not very smart of you, was it, binding yourself to one like that. Letting her wolves get at you?"

Rook breathed out a sigh of relief. So he didn't have to explain. "It was stupid, yes," he agreed.

"You were trying to save that idiot Finn!" Tatter put in, from where he sat in his nest of blankets. "Not stupid at all, dear Rook."

"Finn is the horse Phouka now, and he's not come back to us, has he?" Rip said.

"He hasn't, no," Asher agreed. His red eyes watched Rook carefully. "Instead of coming home to us he's staying with that new Lady, the one who somehow managed to defeat the Mór even though she's no more than a girl."

Rook nodded. He didn't add anything, because the less he said about Fer, the better.

Asher straightened and stepped closer. "But Rook, it's been ages since the Mór lost her bid to be a Lady. What've you been up to since then?"

The question he'd been dreading. "This and that," Rook mumbled.

"Really!" Asher exclaimed.

Beside him, Rip rose to his feet. His black and red

body paint made him look like a creature of shadow and burning coals. His eyes gleamed orange in his black-painted face.

"This and that, is it?" Asher went on. He glanced at Rip and gave a slight nod. "We heard *this*"—Rip reached out and gave Rook a rough shove. Asher went on, leaning closer. "You've spent the last little while skulking 'round the borders of that new Lady-girl's lands, and we've heard *that*"—Rip shoved harder, and Rook stumbled back, his heart pounding—"you gave a ride to a nathe's messenger but didn't bring his message to us, as you should have."

Rip shoved with both hands and, as Rook crashed to the cave floor, Rip flicked his shifter-tooth into his mouth, blurring into his dog shape. Rook scrambled backward as Rip came snarling after him. A heavy leap, and Rip forced him to the ground, breathing down on him with two big paws on his chest. Panting, Rook stared up. The Rip-dog had a heavy muzzle and small eyes, and he growled deep in his chest. His breath was hot and smelled of dead rabbits. Rook lifted an arm to push the dog off; Rip seized his wrist in his teeth. Rook froze.

Asher crouched next to him. Firelight gleamed from the crystals knotted into his braids. "What we hear is, you brought the nathe message to the girl instead." He grinned. "So. What's going on, Rook?"

Rook shook his head. Not telling.

Rip bit harder, his teeth digging into Rook's skin.

"Get off me, Rip," Rook growled.

Asher's eyes narrowed. After a moment he stood and gave his sideways nod to Rip, and the dog released his grip.

Rook got shakily to his feet, rubbing his wrist. Rip's teeth had left indentations but hadn't drawn blood.

"Ah, Rook." Tatter loomed up beside him and before Rook could flinch away, put a comforting hand on his head. "We raised you from a baby, didn't we? You've always been a strange one, but we know what you're thinking."

"That's right, we do," Asher said, coming up on Rook's other side. He shot Rook a sideways grin. "That girl's got some kind of binding magic. She used it on Phouka, and now she's trying to use it on you. But you're a puck, after all. Come on and tell us the rest, and we'll help you get free of her."

Rook held himself stiffly away from them.

Fer? Binding magic? Is that what it was—not friendship but magic?

"Come on," Asher said again gently, then whispered, *"Brother."*

Rook gave a shaky sigh. He was a puck, and they

were his brother-pucks; they knew him better than any-body. And maybe they were right. He gave in, leaning his head against Tatter's shoulder. He'd tell them every-thing, and it would be all right.

four

The bees that she couldn't understand were a problem, and the oaths were a huge problem, and still another problem was the glamorie.

Fer sat cross-legged on the bed in her room. During the summer, the Lady's house, built on a platform high in the Lady Tree, was just a wood-shingled roof with walls made of billowing green silk curtains weighted at the bottom with river stones. On the floor was a green and gold rug with a pattern of leaves woven into it, and next to her bed was a wooden chest where she kept her clothes and the box her father had made out of pale wood, her leafy crown wrapped in blue silk cloth, and a broken black arrow fletched with crow feathers.

On top of the chest was a smooth, shallow wooden

bowl, and in the bowl was the glamorie.

After the defeated Mór had turned into a giant crow and fled from the land, Fer had found the glamorie the Mór had stolen from Laurelin. The Mór had worn the stolen glamorie for two reasons, Fer figured. One, to hide what she truly was—a fierce crow-woman hunter and not a Lady at all—and two, to force her people to love and obey her. Even Fer had almost fallen under the glamorie's spell, and she didn't trust it one bit.

The glamorie had looked like a tattered bit of cobweb in the grass after it had dropped off the Mór. Fer hadn't even noticed it; one of the wolf-guards had picked it up and saved it for her. The first time she'd touched it, the glamorie had made her fingers tingle and turn cold. Fer had put it in the wooden bowl and had tried to forget about it.

But she was going to the nathe to convince the High Ones that she was the true Lady of the Summerlands, like her mother before her. There would be a competition, one she absolutely had to win. To do that she would need all the power and magic at her command, and that meant using the glamorie.

Fer climbed off the bed. In the bowl, the glamorie didn't look like shredded cobweb anymore. Even in the greenish light of the room, it looked like a silver net, shimmering with pearl and ice and moonlight.

Carefully Fer reached into the bowl. The glamorie felt cold under her fingers. With one quick motion, she grabbed it, flung it up in the air, and stepped under it as it fell. She shivered as the silver net settled over her. She blinked, and it had disappeared. But she still felt it, icy against her skin and a little prickly. Uncomfortable.

What was the glamorie, exactly? If she looked in a mirror, what would she see? The ordinary Fer, tall and skinny, with her long, honey-colored braid coming unraveled and grass stains on her bare feet? Or would she see a tall, slender princess glowing with power and beauty?

"It looks stupid," said a rough voice from behind her.

She whirled, and there was Rook, crouched just beside the doorway. He was wearing a tattered green shirt now. She frowned at him. When he'd left, it had seemed clear that he wasn't coming back. But here he was.

"Where—" she started. *Where have you been?* she was going to ask.

But she already knew his answer. *None of your business.*

Instead of asking, she held up her arms and turned around, showing him the glamorie. He'd said she looked stupid. "What do you see, Rook?"

He got to his feet, scowling. "I always see the real you, Fer."

That's right, he did. Pucks had clear vision. No magic

or glamorie could enchant them; they always saw straight through to the truth. They spoke the truth too, but only when it would cause the most trouble.

"You'll not wear it, will you?" he asked.

"Maybe," she answered. Or maybe not. Fer raised her arm and tried to see the glamorie against her tan skin. Did her arm look more slender, more graceful? Less knobby at the elbow? She lowered her arm and glanced at Rook. "I thought you said you weren't coming with me," she said.

"So I did." He was still scowling, but down at his bare feet now, instead of at her.

She smiled at him. She really needed a friend with her when she met the High Ones and competed to become the Lady of the Summerlands. "I'm glad you changed your mind."

"Don't be," he muttered. Then his head jerked up.

Fer heard it too, a thump of heavy footsteps on the wooden platform. Behind Rook, a dark shape loomed in the doorway. "Here he is!" the shape called over its shoulder, and then it ducked into the room. Fray. Like all the wolf-guards, she detested Rook.

"Here now, Puck." Fray made a grab after Rook, who ducked under her hands and darted behind Fer. "Sorry, Lady Gwynnefar," Fray said. "He got past us."

A second, older wolf-guard bounded into the room.

"Is it biting time?" he asked.

Behind Fer, Rook growled. "Keep those idiot wolves off me."

"You're not wanted here, Puck," Fray said. She and the other wolf-guard started edging around Fer, watching Rook intently, trying to trap him.

Fer raised her hand. Both of the wolf-guards stopped short, staring at her. Their eyes widened. Fer felt the glamorie spark over her skin, a sudden wash of chilly moonlight.

"Lady," Fray whispered.

Fer caught her breath. What did the wolf-guards see? Power? Magic? She opened her mouth to speak. "It's all right, Fray. Leave the puck to me." Her voice sounded strange. Cold and distant.

"Yes, Lady," Fray murmured.

Her partner bowed his grizzled gray head. "Yes, Lady," he repeated. The two guards shuffled out the door.

"Hmm," Rook said, and stepped up beside her. He was smiling, but not in a nice way. "Maybe you should wear that thing after all."

"No, I shouldn't." Fer bent her head, stripped off the glamorie, shivering a little as the chill lifted from her skin, and tossed it back into the bowl.

It glimmered against the dark wood. Beautiful, yes,

but the glamorie was dangerous, too. She hadn't thought about it before, but—the glamorie affected the people who saw it. Did it also affect the one who was wearing it? The glamorie had been her mother's, so she must have worn it. Had it affected Lady Laurelin, too?

Fer decided. She'd bring the glamorie with her to the nathe, but she wasn't going to wear it unless she absolutely had to.

Besides the glamorie, Fer wasn't sure what to bring with her. Her bow and arrows, for sure. But what else? In their letter, the High Ones had sounded noble and proud, so she needed to look like a Lady. But she didn't have anything fancy to wear. . . .

Rook had faded back to lurk by the door. When she checked again, he was gone. Hopefully he'd stay out of trouble until it was time to go through the Way to the nathe.

After putting the glamorie in the wooden bowl and setting it aside, Fer dug through the chest to see if the Mór had left any clothes behind. She hadn't bothered to look before; she'd just dumped her own clothes on top of what was already there. She pulled out her wooden box of healing herbs and tinctures, then her jeans and T-shirts and sneakers and her patch-jacket, then the layer of the Mór's clothes, black silk shirts and trousers, and a crow feather here and there. Under that was a layer of dried herbs—lavender and something else, maybe artemisia, from the smell of it—and then more clothes, neatly folded. Fer lifted them out and laid them on her bed.

A creamy white shirt with a high collar. A vest embroidered in green silk with oak leaves. A knee-length dark green suede coat, soft as butter, with silver buttons shaped like leaves. Trousers made of some heavier fabric. High boots made of soft leather. Two more shirts like the first one.

Fer ran her hand along the front of the vest. The embroidered leaves felt bumpy under her fingers. Some of the leaves were frayed, and one of the buttons was missing. These were not new clothes. But they weren't the Mór's, either.

Fer blinked away sudden tears. They were her mother's clothes. Laurelin's. She'd never met her mother, only imagined her, and in her dreams she'd been wearing clothes just like these. Not fancy princess dresses, but clothes good for riding and for walking on silent feet through her forest land.

After checking to be sure that Rook was still gone, Fer stripped off her T-shirt and shorts and tried on the silk shirt and the trousers, then pulled on the boots. The vest was too big and the coat's sleeves hung down over her hands. The shirt's high collar brushed her chin and made her feel like standing straight and tall. She looked down at herself.

They were nice, but the clothes were just like the glamorie—neither fit her quite right.

Reaching into the chest again, she took out the silken package and unwrapped it. Freshly budded oak leaves and twigs had been twined into a crown. It looked as fresh and green as it had on the day it'd been set on her head, crowning her Lady of the Summerlands. Brushing tendrils of her hair aside, she put it on. There. She *was* the Lady, and no High One could tell her otherwise.

As she was folding back the too-long coat sleeves, she felt a tingle along a thread that bound her to one of her people, the fox-girl Twig. A moment later, Twig slipped into the room.

Seeing Fer in the new clothes and the crown, Twig gave a shy smile. "Pretty," she said.

Startled, Fer frowned. *Pretty* was not what she was after.

"They were hers," Twig said. With a slender hand, she stroked the coat sleeve. "The Lady Laurelin's—your mother's." She pulled a wooden comb out of the pocket of her shift. "Sit down." She pointed at the bed. "I'll do your hair."

Fer took off the coat, then sat on the bed. Twig's

quick fingers set aside the leafy crown and unraveled her braid; Fer closed her eyes as the comb went through her hair, long, slow strokes.

"It's good to have you back, Lady," Twig murmured. "The land is happier with you here."

Fer smiled. She was happier here too.

"If you would only let us swear our oaths . . . ," Twig began.

Fer sighed and opened her eyes. "Twig," she interrupted. "I have to go see the High Ones at the nathe."

The comb stilled. "Why, Lady?"

"They . . ." She wasn't sure how much to tell. Just talking about it made her feel shaky. "They summoned me. I have to prove to them that I'm the true Lady of these lands."

"We will come too," Twig said, and started combing again.

What did she mean by "we"? Fer felt another thread-pull from one of her people and opened her eyes to see Fray looming in the doorway.

"Yup, we're coming," Fray said, folding her arms.

"No, you're not," Fer said firmly. "Nobody's coming. I'm going by myself."

In the doorway, Fray shook her head. "That puck is going, isn't he?"

"Yes," Fer admitted.

Fray stepped further into the room. "Lady, he's not to be trusted."

She and Rook had risked their lives together to defeat the Mór—she trusted Rook more than she trusted almost anyone. "Rook's my friend."

"He isn't," Fray insisted. "A puck cares only for his brother-pucks. He follows no rules but his own, and a puck's rule is to make trouble wherever he goes. Pucks are betrayers and destroyers." Fray bared her sharp teeth in a snarl. "They are outcast for a reason!"

Fer opened her mouth to argue, when Fray continued.

"Lady Gwynnefar, if that puck's going with you, then we're coming too," the wolf-girl pronounced.

"We're coming," Twig added. Once more she ran the comb through Fer's hair. "You are our Lady." She set down the comb and started to weave the hair into a braid. "We have to come."

five

Rook lurked at the edge of the clearing, hand in a pocket of his shorts, the shifter-tooth and shifter-bone warming under his fingers. The sun was setting, the long, rosy twilight of midsummer. Shadows gathered under the trees, and fireflies flashed and floated in the air.

On the other side of the clearing, he saw Fer standing next to Phouka, who had once been Finn and a puck like Rook but was stuck now in his black-maned, fiery-eyed horse form. Fer was dressed in a shirt, shorts, and bare feet, and she wore her patched jacket on top, the one stitched with protective spells. Her hair hung in its usual long braid down her back. A swarm of bees circled her head, humming. She reached out and patted Phouka's neck but kept her eyes on the sky.

She was waiting, Rook knew, for the first star to appear. The Way in and out of this land began in the clearing, and it could only be opened at the turning of the day into night, or of night into day.

The Ways were like that—tricksy. Most Ways were like unlocked doors that stayed open all the time and could be used by anyone, even the pucks. A few Ways opened only on the longest or shortest day of the year. Some, like this one, could only be opened at certain times of day or night. The Way that went to the human world, where there was no magic, could be opened only by a Lord or a Lady, or by one of the High Ones.

Anybody could go through this Way to the nathe, where there was a meeting of all Ways, but a puck on his own would never get inside the nathe. The guards there would stop him from coming in.

Near Fer were her wolf-guards, all prick-eared and hackle-raised now that they'd spotted him in his patch of shadow. More of Fer's people gave him fearful glances and edged away, keeping Fer and the guards between themselves and him.

He felt a growl rising in his chest when he saw the fox-girls, Burr and Twig, flinch away. Afraid of him. Well, they should be; he was a puck, after all.

He'd woken up that morning in the puck cave in the Foglands, tangled in a warm, sleepy heap with the other pucks, some of them in their dog forms, others lying sprawled by the dying fire. Scrap, the baby, was curled against his chest in his puppy form. Home with the other pucks, where he belonged; how he'd missed it, especially his littlest brother.

And here he was, back in Fer's land again.

Asher had gotten the whole story out of him. Rook had told him and Tatter and Rip about how he'd sworn a thrice-binding oath to the Mór and how Fer had defeated the Mór by refusing to spill more blood in the land. And about the other thing.

"*Three* times?" Asher had asked, appalled. "You let that girl save your life three times?"

"I didn't *let* her," Rook snapped. She'd just done it. First she'd saved him from the wolves, who would've torn him to pieces on the Mór's orders. Then she'd kept him on Phouka's back during a wild ride through the Way, when to fall off would've meant dissolving into dust. And then she'd healed him when the wolf bites had turned him feverish and would have killed him, like as not.

Asher's eyes narrowed. "What did you give her for it?"

"Nothing," Rook shot back.

"You haven't made her any promises, sworn to do

her a service, bound yourself to her, nothing like that?" Asher asked.

"I told you—no."

"But she knows you're a puck and she lets you come and go as you will, is that it?" Asher went on.

"She does, yes," Rook admitted.

"So, she's a fool," Asher mused.

Maybe she was, trusting a puck. Calling him her *friend*.

Then Asher had gotten a keen look in his orange-bright eyes. "We can use this to our advantage, can't we, brothers?"

Rip, in his dog form, had growled. Tatter grinned and nodded. And then they'd come up with a plan, a devious and tricksy puck-plan to bring trouble to the High Ones and to get back at Lady Gwynnefar for stealing Phouka away from them. "And you, dear Rook," Asher had said, "are the one who is going to make it happen."

So, like it or not, back he'd come. Fer would get him into the nathe, and then he'd carry out his brother-pucks' plan.

Across the clearing, Fer looked like she was arguing with her wolf-guard. The big young female folded her burly arms and shook her head, saying no. Fer stepped closer and pointed toward the forest, in the direction of the Lady Tree. Ah. Fer wanted the guard to stay behind. That would make things easier, having no idiot wolf-guards around.

Rook narrowed his eyes, watching to see if she'd put on the glamorie to force the wolf-girl to obey her.

Then the wolf-guard pointed across the clearing, straight at him. Fer looked over, and seeing Rook, her face brightened. "Hi, Rook," she called.

Her people fell silent at that, and, as he crossed the clearing toward her and Phouka, they edged deeper into the shadows. As if he wouldn't see them cowering there. Stupid.

When he reached Fer, the girl wolf-guard stepped forward, blocking him.

"Back off," Rook snarled. He felt in his pocket for his shifter-tooth. She was younger than the other guards; in his dog form he'd be able to give her a good fight.

The wolf-guard leaned over him and showed her teeth. "Watch your manners, Puck," she growled.

Rook barked out a sharp laugh. "Oh, sure I will." He ducked past the guard and gave Fer a mock bow. "Lady Gwynnefar," he said. There. How was that for manners?

Fer gave him a sunny smile, as if his coming along to the nathe made her happy.

Her happiness to see him made him feel prickly. "Are

the idiot wolves coming too?" he asked.

"Just Fray," she answered, nodding at the young female. "Who is not an *idiot*. And Twig," she added, pointing at the fox-girl, who was strapping Fer's bow and quiver of arrows to the saddle of her own mount, a white goat with curly horns. "The rest are staying behind. Except Phouka." Fer rested her hand on the horse's neck.

Phouka watched Rook with flame-yellow eyes. Almost like he suspected Rook of something too. Rook grinned at him, and Phouka stamped his hoof in reply and snorted. Phouka knew his brother-puck well enough to know he was up to no good.

"It's time, Rook," Fer said with a glance at the sky. He could tell she was nervous by the way the bees whirled around her head. She was right to be nervous, being summoned by the High Ones like this. They would feel no friendship toward a half-human girl; he knew that much.

The sky had grown dark; just a shadow of pink and gray lingered in the west, where the sun had set. "Will you be able to keep up with us?" Fer asked him.

As an answer, he reached into his pocket, pulling out the shifter-bone, which he popped into his mouth. The feeling of the change washed over him, his hands and feet hardening into hooves, his back lengthening, his mane and tail flying free, and a blink later he stood beside Fer, a black horse with yellow eyes, stamping and snorting and ready to run.

Fer stood staring at him, wide-eyed. She'd never seen him shift into a horse before. Good. Maybe that would help her remember that he was a puck, and not some tame thing.

Then she looked away. A star had appeared in the sky, a spark hovering just over the trees. "Come on," she said. Her bees zoomed around the clearing and then shot away, toward the star.

Phouka, taller and broader, shoved Rook aside with his shoulder. Fer grabbed Phouka's mane and swung herself onto his back. The wolf-guard, carrying a sack over her shoulder, climbed up after her, and they clung to Phouka's back as he reared. He hit the ground running, straight toward the star, and Rook pounded after them with the fox-girl and her mount falling into line behind him.

Stay close to the new Lady, Asher had ordered. *Get through to the nathe.*

On through the forest they raced, dodging trees, twigs swiping across their faces, leaves and bushes and ferns blurring into a swirl of green and darkness. Ahead, Fer clung to Phouka's mane and lifted her other hand, waving it to the side as if she was brushing aside a curtain. Opening the Way.

Rook followed Phouka as he leaped, and they shot like arrows through the night, toward the star, which flew toward them, a bolt of lightning-brightness that was suddenly all around them.

six

Fer felt the change as Phouka's hooves left the ground and swung up into the Way. She felt Fray's strong arms around her and knew the wolf-guard would not fall off. Beside them, Rook galloped with his mane and tail streaming behind him. Farther back, Twig and her goat-mount raced through the blinding star-whiteness.

Squinting, Fer spotted a shape like a glass globe hurtling through the air toward them; a blink, and the shape was a whole world, and then Phouka's hoofs landed like feathers settling on short, emerald-green grass.

Rook, still in his horse form, trotted up beside her, his ears pricked.

Behind them lay a wide lake gleaming in the summer sun like a huge silver mirror enclosed by low green hills.

Was this it? The nathe? It felt strange. The air was warm, but with ribbons of freezing cold twisting through it.

Lots of Ways opened here, she realized, in the lake. Ways to other lands like her own Summerlands, and—she could feel it like a shiver under her skin—to the human world. That would make sense, for the High Ones to live at the meeting of all Ways. She felt a tingling in her own hands and looked down at them. They looked ordinary—long fingers, ragged nails, a scabby scrape on the back of one she'd gotten climbing the Lady Tree. Her hands felt full of power, though, as if she could reach out in this place and sweep open all the Ways and step through to any land or any other world.

That was good, the power feeling. It might help her prove to the High Ones that she was the true Lady of the Summerlands. She clenched her hands around the power, as if she could hold on to it, so it would be there when she needed it.

Phouka snorted and stamped. Fer patted his neck and slid to the ground, which felt solid under her feet. She turned and saw, about twenty paces from the silver lake, what looked like a high wall. Fer walked closer to see it better. It *was* a wall, but it was made of leafy vines as thick as her wolf-guard Fray's burly arms. The vines were woven tightly together and they pulsed like bulging veins.

Overhead, the sky was the silver color of the lake, with lighter clouds drifting across it. A glassy sun leaned toward the west. The grass under her feet gleamed, as if tipped with crystal. The air seemed to glitter with a cold light, even though the breeze was warm.

"Is this it?" asked Rook, sounding doubtful.

Fer looked aside to see that he'd shifted from his horse form and stood with his hands on his hips, staring at the wall. Keeping their distance from him stood Fray, Twig, and Twig's goat-mount. The waning sun cast their shadows long upon the ground.

"This has to be it," Fer muttered to herself. It was where the bees had led them. But there wasn't any way to get in, at least not that she could see. The weird thing was, the vine-wall didn't curve, the way it would if it were built around something. It just went straight on in both directions.

Now what?

Her bees hovered over her head, weaving a pattern and speaking to her in a low grumble-hum. *Hmmmzmmm*. She still couldn't understand what they were saying, but they didn't seem angry or upset. Fer stepped closer to the wall, and the vines swelled as if the net was tightening, determined to keep her out.

"Careful, Lady," Fray said.

"Careful," echoed Twig softly.

"It's all right," Fer murmured. She felt again the power in her hands—a Lady's power for opening Ways—and reached out to rest a hand on one of the ropy vines. It felt rough under her fingers, and clammy. The same tingly feeling she got when opening a Way swept through her. Blinking, she stepped back and wiped her fingers on her shorts.

After a moment, the vines twitched and pulled apart like a curtain rippling open, and three people stepped out right in front of her. All three were tall and as slender as willow trees, with rough brown skin and greenish-blond hair, two men and a woman. They wore embroidered coats and boots that reminded Fer of her mother's fine clothes, the ones she had packed in saddlebags on the back of Twig's mount. They were well armed, with long knives in sheaths at their belts and bows and quivers of arrows slung over their shoulders. Guards, then.

The willow-woman stepped closer and looked Fer up and down with glittering green eyes. Her lip curled a little as she surveyed Fer's patch-jacket and shorts and bare feet, but her eyes widened seeing the bees that hovered over her head.

"We greet you," the willow-woman said with a graceful nod that Fer guessed really should have been a bow, to be proper. "You are Gwynnefar?"

Fer frowned. They hadn't called her *Lady Gwynnefar.*

Not a good sign. She found her voice. "Yes, I am."

"We are nathe-wardens," the willow-woman went on. "We serve the High Ones and we are to welcome you to this place." She looked past her at Fray and Twig. "These are your servants?"

Fer opened her mouth to say no, when Fray interrupted.

"She's our Lady," Fray said, folding her burly arms. Twig nodded, and folded her skinny arms too.

"Very well," the warden said. She examined them again, this time looking more carefully at Rook. She frowned, and her hand went to the knife at her belt. "What is that creature?"

"Don't you know a puck when you see one?" Rook said, grinning.

As Rook spoke, one of the willow-men whipped out his knife. "That's the puck who attacked me and stole the High Ones' letter!"

The other two nathe-wardens unslung their bows and jerked arrows from their quivers. Rook thrust his hand into the pocket of his shorts, grabbing for his shifter-tooth.

It was going to get bloody. "Stop!" Fer shouted, and stepped between them with her hands raised.

The wardens froze with their bows half-drawn. The other willow-man gripped his knife.

"The puck is my friend." Her bees zoomed in a wider arc, circling around Rook and then back to her, weaving golden patterns against the silver sky.

"Ah," the nathe-warden said with a sneer. "So the puck is tame, is he?"

In an instant, Rook's hand flashed from his pocket, the shifter-tooth was in his mouth, and a huge black dog lunged past Fer, knocking the warden to the grass. Her bow went flying. Rook put his paws on the warden's shoulders and snarled into her face.

Rook spat the tooth out and became a boy again. "No," he growled down at the nathe-warden. "Not tame." He climbed off the guard, shoving his shifter-tooth back into his pocket.

The warden snatched up her bow and got to her feet. "This puck is unbound," she hissed, "with allegiance to none but his own kind." She fit an arrow to the bow-string and drew it back. Her eyes were keen, sighting down the arrow, straight at Rook's heart. "He will *not* be admitted."

"Just wait a minute," Fer said, and turned and stepped between the wardens and Rook. If they loosed their arrows, they'd shoot her in the back. "That wasn't exactly helpful, Rook," she said softly. "But if you want to come with me, I won't leave you behind. Do you still want to come?"

He hesitated. Then, "I do, yes."

Why did he want to come, that was the question. Was it really to cause trouble? He *was* a puck, after all. He'd been very careful to remind her of that. And she had both Grand-Jane's and Fray's warnings about pucks to consider.

But Rook was her truest friend. He hadn't done anything to change that. Not yet, anyway.

She looked straight into his eyes. She was taking a big risk, and she wanted him to know it. "They could turn me away, and then I won't be able to prove to them that I'm the true Lady of the Summerlands."

He scowled. "Don't put that on me, Fer. It's your choice."

"I know," she answered. "I choose to trust you." She turned back to the wardens. "You're right that the puck is not bound to me by an oath. He's here because he is my friend. Will you let him in?"

The leader of the nathe-wardens hesitated. "This is an unheard of thing, for a puck to be allowed into the nathe." Then she lowered her bow. "But we are under orders to admit you for the competition, so we have no choice. If you will be responsible for this puck's actions, he will be admitted."

Fer took a deep breath, hoping she wasn't about to make a big mistake. "I do take responsibility for him."

"Very well." The nathe-warden slid her arrow back into its quiver; then she turned and motioned gracefully at the opening in the vine-wall. The other two wardens moved aside. "Come," she said. "Enter."

Fer stepped into the nathe.

seven

Rook was about to follow Fer and her people through the opening in the vine-wall when two of the nathewardens grabbed him, and from behind, the other one looped her arm across Rook's throat.

"Puck," the warden hissed into his ear.

He struggled, but their arms were like supple willow branches—too strong.

"Get off," he gasped.

The warden choking him increased the pressure. He twisted in their grip, then went limp, hoping to fool them into relaxing their hold, but they didn't let go. Curse it, were they going to kill him? He hadn't even done anything yet! Black spots swam in front of his eyes.

The warden behind him loosened her arm, and Rook

caught a breath. He felt a sharp jab at his back through his shirt—a knife.

"We know you're no friend of that part-human girl, no matter what she says," the warden hissed, her breath hot in Rook's ear. "Pucks are friends to none but their own. We know you're here to bring trouble. If we catch you, Puck, you're dead."

The wardens let him go with a shove, and he went stumbling through the opening in the vine-wall. He whirled to glare at the nathe-wardens.

They stalked coolly past, one of them resheathing his knife.

These wardens knew their business. And they meant what they'd said about killing him. Tricky. He'd have to be extra careful.

Behind him, the vines twisted together, sealing them all inside. "The problem with a place like this," Rook muttered to himself, "is that it might not be so easy to get back out again."

It was in a puck's blood to not like being closed in anywhere. There had been too many times when a Lord or Lady had discovered what they called a "nest of pucks" in their land and had sent warriors to burn them out and hunt them down, if they could catch them. So pucks always found a way out—a way to escape—if they had to.

He eyed the wall. It was high, but it looked climbable.

He knew what he had to do, now that he'd gotten in. Nathe-wardens or not, it should be easy enough to slip away and get started on his brothers' puckish plan.

But things were already getting more complicated than he would like. He'd felt a strange pull in his chest when Fer had called him her friend, and it had gotten stronger when she'd stepped between him and the drawn bows of the nathe-wardens. It was as if a thread had spun itself out from her heart to tie him to her. Maybe his brother-pucks were right, and Fer did have some kind of binding magic.

He was a puck. He would not be bound to Fer, not by an oath, and not by anything else, either, including friendship. Concentrating, and growling in the back of his throat, he snapped the thread in his heart.

Fer and the rest had gone on ahead, but one of her bees bumbled against his ear. The buzz sounded loud, almost as if the bee was trying to tell him something. He brushed it away before it could sting him, and followed.

So far the nathe was forest, but not a clean, open forest like Fer's land. Here the trees were thick and gnarled, ancient and crowded together, and, as evening drew on, darkness gathered in their branches. The trees grew in an absolutely straight line, as if they'd just stepped back to

make a path, and they'd close in again once Fer and her
people had passed. Their branches met overhead so it was
as if they were walking through a darkening green tunnel. The air was damp and smelled strange. He sniffed,
knowing his dog-nose would make more sense of it. It
smelled old, that was it. And stuffy.

It made the hair on the back of his neck stand up. The
forest seemed to be closing in around him, and no puck
liked to be stuck in a place he couldn't get out of, especially a place like this.

※ ※ ※

Fer set aside her worry about bringing Rook into the
nathe. She'd keep an eye on him and ask Fray to watch
him too, but she had other, more important things to
deal with right now.

Even though it wasn't hers, she could feel this land.
The grass on the path tickled her bare feet, and below that
she felt the land's stillness. It was old, and it didn't like
change. It didn't like her, either. The oak trees along the
path seemed to lean over her, threatening and so ancient
that she was like a firefly to them, a brief flash of life that
would be gone soon enough. Still, they wanted her gone
now; they could sense she was partly human, and that
meant she was no kin of the ones who lived here.

Fer shivered and followed the wardens deeper into
the nathe.

It was early evening, the same time that she'd left the Summerlands when the first stars were appearing. On down the path they went, the forest gloomy and silent all around them. Her bees, hovering just over her left shoulder, sounded very loud in the stillness. Then, up ahead, she spied what looked like a huge storm cloud massing above the thickly gathered trees.

No, it was gray and mossy—like a low mountain.

As they got closer, the path ended and the forest opened onto a wide lawn, and she saw that it wasn't a storm cloud or a mountain.

"The nathe," said one of the nathe-guards, with a sweeping bow. "The home of the High Ones, and the place where all the Lords and Ladies are gathering to witness the contest that will decide the next Lord or Lady of the Summerlands."

Hearing them talk about the competition like that made Fer's stomach clench. She didn't even know yet what kind of contest it would be. Well, she had come here to win, and that's what she would do. She took a steadying breath and looked where the guards were pointing.

In the gray light of evening, the nathe loomed dark over the lawn, steep-sided like a castle, with towers that reached into the night sky like piled clouds. But it wasn't made out of stone, Fer realized, as they circled the lawn on a narrow path paved with white pebbles. The nathe looked like it had grown up out of the ground, as if it had been there for thousands and thousands of years. As they got closer, she saw, by the light of torches set along a courtyard before it, that the nathe was covered with moss and rough, gray bark; gray, leafy vines pulsed across its walls in places, like veins. Like the outer wall they'd met at the edge of this land. Maybe it really *had* grown here, a castle-sized, mossy tree stump. Maybe it had roots that went way down into the ground.

She realized that she'd stopped, staring, and Rook waited beside her. Behind them stood Twig and Fray.

"I don't like the look of this place," Rook muttered.

The nathe was strange, Fer thought, but it wasn't really scary. Many windows that reminded her of gleaming cats' eyes peered out of the bark walls; they weren't square, like regular windows, but oblong and gnarled, as if the walls had grown around them. The towers grew straight, like stubby tree trunks lopped off at the top, with no branches. Gnarled, rooty stairways led from many doorways down to the courtyard, which was bustling with people coming and going.

"Come," said the warden, and waved her hand toward the nathe. "It grows late. I will show you and your people—and the puck—to your rooms."

Fer started to follow, when she heard a sharp whinny.

Turning, she saw that one of the wardens had started leading away Twig's curly-horned goat. Phouka was standing with all four hooves planted, refusing to go.

"Do not worry," the warden said, gliding to Fer's side. "They will be well looked after in the High Ones' stables."

Fer stepped closer to the horse. "Is that okay, Phouka?" she whispered, and rested her hand against his neck. "I don't think you can get in there." She pointed at the looming nathe before them.

Phouka tossed his head, then pranced across the court-yard after the warden and the white goat. With a wave of her hand, Fer sent most of her bees after them, but kept one bee with her. It circled her head, then drifted down to cling to the collar of her patch-jacket. She heard it humming quietly to itself.

Tomorrow she'd have to find out where the stables were and check on Phouka and the bees. But now her feet were sore and she was more than ready for some dinner.

"All right," Fer said, and she let the warden lead her and Fray and Twig, with Rook trailing behind, up a winding set of stairs in the side of the nathe. The door was like the windows she'd seen, oval-shaped and look-ing like the bark had grown around it. Rook stepped warily through, as if he thought it was going to snap closed behind him.

The warden led them along winding tunnels that looked like they'd been hollowed out and polished. The wood was smooth and cool under her bare feet. The tunnels were lit not by torches—fire wasn't a good idea in a castle made out of wood, Fer figured—but by glowing crystals set in niches in the walls. Now and then they passed an arched door or another hallway leading off, and they passed lots of important-looking people who stared as they went by, until they arrived at a door where two other wardens waited. A nod to them and the warden went on, leading them up a stairway that got narrower as it wound up and up, into one of the trunklike towers

At last they reached the top of the stairs. Fer caught her breath and surveyed the room the warden had shown her into. It was round and had been hollowed and smoothed out of the nathe wood, just like the tunnels. The walls, ceiling, and floor were the dark brown color of polished mahogany, and many crystals set in niches made the room bright, though the light cast sharp shadows. A low table was set before plump, green-covered pillows big enough to sit on, like chairs. Three doors led off from the main room.

"Dinner will be brought to you shortly," the warden

said from the doorway. "Do not leave these rooms, for the nathe has many winding ways, and it is easy to become lost."

Hm. She wasn't going to let them keep her in these rooms like a prisoner. "I want to see the High Ones," she said, trying to put some Ladylike snap into her words.

"You will be sent for later this evening. That will give you time"—the warden paused and looked down her nose at Fer—"to dress." And with another graceful bow, she left, closing the door behind her.

This evening, then. Fer nodded. Good. The High Ones weren't wasting any time.

Twig carried in the saddlebags she'd taken from her mount, and Fray stood stolidly in the doorway with the rest of the packs. Rook pushed past them and circled the main room, then went prowling into one of the others.

Fray followed Rook into the room; then she shoved him out its door. "This one's mine," the wolf-guard said. "There's a bed in here for you too," she said to Twig, and went back in, carrying the packs. Twig followed her with the bags. Growling, Rook went to inspect the other rooms.

When he came back, Fer had flopped onto one of the pillows, feeling in her bones the tiredness from the ride and the long walk through the forest. The bee had settled on the top of her head, almost as if it was tired too.

She lifted her bare foot; it was dirty and grass-stained. She'd need a bath if she was going to see the High Ones later. Her stomach rumbled. "I hope they bring dinner soon," she said.

Rook paced around the edges of the room.

"What's the matter?" Fer asked him.

He gave her a quick, flame-eyed glance, then resumed his pacing.

"Well?" she prompted.

"There aren't any windows, did you notice?" he said, coming to stand before her.

She checked the smoothly polished walls. He was right; there weren't.

"No way out," he said shortly. He wrapped his arms around his chest, as if trying to keep himself from pacing again.

She climbed off the pillow and pointed at the door. "There's the way out."

"It's guarded," he shot back.

"Does this look like a prison to you?" She waved her hand at the room.

"That door could grow over," Rook said darkly, "and we'd be sealed in."

"Oh, Rook," she said, and smiled at him. He glowered back.

A knock at the door interrupted them, and then it

opened, and a parade of short, sticklike people were ush-
ered in by a warden. They had grayish skin and tufts
of green leaves on their heads, and they carried platters
almost as big as they were, covered with dishes and food,
which they wordlessly set on the low table. Then, bowing, they left.

"There!" Fer said, kneeling by the table. "Dinner."

She, Fray, and Twig ate while Rook prowled restlessly
around the room.

Then she got ready to meet the High Ones.

eight

After having a bath, Fer stepped out of her room. Twig had braided her hair, and she'd put on her usual plain shirt, jeans, sneakers, and patched jacket. She carried a pile of clothes, which she set on the low table, along with the small wooden box with the glamorie in it.

That will give you time to dress, the warden had said in her snooty way. As if Fer's ordinary clothes weren't good enough.

"What do you think, Rook?" she asked. "I have these other clothes, and I could wear them instead." She unfolded them, showing him her mother's fine green coat and vest and silk shirt and high leather boots.

Rook looked uneasy, standing by the only door

leading out of the room. "You look well enough as you are," he answered.

"No 'stupid glamorie,' then," she added, shaking the little box.

"Definitely not." He shook his head.

She shot him a quick smile, and he gave her a twitchy grin in return.

"You should wear it, Fer-Lady," Twig piped up from the doorway to Fer's room. "The High Ones are very fine."

"No, Rook is right," Fer said, setting the box back on the table. "The glamorie doesn't fit me very well."

A knock on the door, and the same nathe-warden, the willow-woman with the greeny-blond hair, stepped inside. "Gwynnefar, you are summoned," she said.

Fer gulped down a sudden surge of nervousness. With a flick of a finger, she called her bee to her, and it clung like a fat gold button to the front of her patch-jacket. She and Fray and Rook followed the warden out of their rooms and down the twisting staircase, then through the tunnel-like hallways. They cut through a long, echoing gallery full of shadows, went up more stairs, and finally arrived at a tall, ornately carved door. Fer put her hand into her patch-jacket pocket and gripped the cloth bag of spelled herbs her grandma had given her. For luck.

"You may enter," the nathe-warden said, and stepped

aside, opening the door wider. Fer went in, followed by Fray and Rook.

The room looked a lot like her own room in the nathe-palace, but bigger and grander and brimming with light.

And it had plenty of windows, she couldn't help but notice.

Sprawling on one of the cushions was a boy who looked about Rook's age, a couple of years older than she was. As Fer stepped into the room, he leaped to his feet, smiling. Fer blinked, dazzled. He was beautiful. The most beautiful person she'd ever seen. He was tall and graceful and golden, with warm brown skin, and tawny hair, and eyes as bright as bronze coins.

Glamorie, she reminded herself. To be that glorious, he had to be wearing a glamorie to disguise his true self. She had another useful thing in her patch-jacket pocket, a flat, round gray stone with a hole in the middle of it, the seeing-stone her father had left her. If she peered through the hole, the stone showed things as they truly were. She gripped it, and it felt cool and smooth under her fingers. Just knowing it was there helped her look away from the beautiful-appearing boy.

"Greetings!" the boy said with a broad smile. "Gwynnefar! I've heard so much about you. So many interesting stories!"

She couldn't help but smile back. Then she reminded herself of her business here. She'd been summoned, after all. "Are you one of the High Ones?" she asked. Somehow she'd expected someone older.

"Ah, no, I am not." The happy smile turned into an exaggerated frown. "I have been so longing to meet you that I could not wait. See, I have sweets for you, and tea." He waved at the table, which was covered with neatly arranged, delicate-looking treats on silver plates.

"Oh." For a second, Fer felt like the floor had been sucked away from under her feet. She'd been expecting to meet the High Ones and learn about the competition, and instead here was this beautiful boy offering her pastries and cream cakes. She shook her head. "Who are you, then?"

His golden eyes twinkled, and he was smiling again. "It is well to be prepared before meeting the High Ones. I want to help, you see! You must ask me any questions so you will be ready."

Leaving Fray and Rook standing by the door, Fer followed the boy to the table, where he draped himself gracefully across a pillow.

He still hadn't answered her question. She stood looking down at him. "Who are you?" she asked again. Once more, and her asking it three times would mean he would have no choice but to answer.

The boy waved an airy hand. "My name is Arenthiel."

He smiled. "But you must call me Aren, because we are going to be good friends, you and I. May I call you Gwynnefar?"

Her real, true name was Fer. That's what Rook called her. She glanced over her shoulder at Rook, who looked like a scruffy, dark smudge in the bright room.

Fer opened her mouth to tell Arenthiel he could call her Fer too, but he interrupted.

"Oh, Gwynnefar!" He jumped to his feet again, and took Fer's hand, pulling her over to Rook. "I see you have brought your puck with you!"

"I'm not—" Rook started.

"Of course you're not!" Arenthiel said, laughing. "You're your own puck, I can see that very well." He gave Fer a secret smile, as if they were sharing some joke, and then looked Rook up and down. "What's his name?" he asked.

Fer opened her mouth to answer.

"Robin," Rook put in, scowling.

Fer closed her mouth. Robin. The name Rook gave to people he didn't trust.

Aren's golden eyes glittered. "Robin. Of course." He turned to Fer. "He's just a puppy, isn't he, Gwynnefar?"

Fer blinked. "I don't know," she said. "Is he?"

"Oh, yes, I should say so," Aren said. "Very young, even for a puck."

"I lost my puppy teeth a long time ago," Rook growled. Fer saw his hand starting toward his pocket, where he kept his shifter-tooth.

Uh-oh. If he shifted into a dog, there would be trouble. "Rook—" she warned.

Then Fray's big hand came down on Rook's shoulder, and she jerked him back. "Don't even think about it, Puck," the wolf-guard said.

Rook clenched his hands into fists.

"Oh, the little puppy is so fierce!" Aren said, still smiling. He spun on his heel and wafted back to the table. "Would you like tea, Gwynnefar?" he asked, and started pouring what looked like cool mint tea into a silver cup.

"Behave yourself," Fer whispered to the still-scowling Rook, and followed Arenthiel back to the table. She still didn't really know who he was. Gingerly she sat on the edge of a cushion.

The glittering boy handed her the teacup with a graceful nod. "Now, ask me questions." He smiled, and she felt his beauty catch her up, like a net.

Fer got hold of herself. This Arenthiel might not like this question, but if he really did want to be her friend she had to ask it. She pulled the seeing-stone out of her pocket and held it up so he could see it. "Is it okay if I look at you with this?" she asked.

His smile didn't falter. "Of course you may! Friends

should not keep secrets from each other." He nodded meaningfully toward Rook.

Fer frowned. Was Rook keeping secrets from her? Shaking her head to get rid of that thought, Fer held the seeing-stone up to her eye. It made the room look very bright. Carefully she examined Arenthiel. Aren.

Strange. He looked just the same. So he wasn't using a glamorie, he really was that compellingly, perfectly beautiful. She lowered the stone. "Thanks," she said.

He raised his teacup to his lips and smiled as he took a sip.

Okay. Well, she did have questions. She opened her mouth to ask about the competition and the High Ones, when he interrupted. Again.

After a quick glance at the door where Rook was standing, he lowered his voice. "One of the things they say about you, Gwynnefar, is that you have bound this puck to you with a thrice-sworn oath. This is such a rare and unusual thing that I simply had to ask you about it."

Rook again! Why was Arenthiel so interested in him? Fer shook her head. "No, that was the Mór, not me."

"Oh!" Aren set down his teacup. "I must have been misinformed. Then he has been tamed, somehow?"

She *really* didn't want to talk about Rook right now. "No," she answered. "He's my friend." Then she went on quickly, "Will I see the High Ones tomorrow?"

"You will!" Aren said brightly. "So let me have a look at you," he said, leaping from his pillow, coming around the table, and pulling Fer to her feet. "Hmmm," he said, studying her.

"What?" Fer asked, starting to feel nervous again. What did he see?

"Oh yes, very nice." He circled, looking her up and down. "Yes," he went on musingly. "The patched coat is simple, yet, somehow, perfect. You must wear it in the competition." He came to stand in front of her. "Now, do you have a glamorie?"

"Yes," she answered. "But I don't like it."

"Oh, that is well," Aren said, smiling. He pulled her down onto a cushion, close beside him. "Trust me," he whispered confidingly. "If you expect to win the competition to become the new Lady of the Summerlands, you must not wear the glamorie. The High Ones will think you are cheating if you do. You must appear as your true self. Come. Promise me you'll not wear your glamorie. Will you promise me that?"

That was an easy promise to make, and it sounded like good advice. "All right," Fer said to her new friend. "I won't wear the glamorie."

✸ ✸ ✸

Rook frowned. Over by the table, Fer and the golden boy sat with their heads together, whispering. The boy wasn't wearing a glamorie, he could see that much with his keen puck vision. But there was something strange about him. Something not quite right.

The boy put his arm around Fer's shoulder and whispered something into her ear. *Aren*, she called him. As if they were friends.

Rook narrowed his eyes, studying the golden boy. The sense of wrongness grew even stronger. Something about him made the hair stand up on the back of his neck. He concentrated, and then he saw it.

The boy looked like a boy, and he wanted Fer to think he was young like her—a friend. But Rook was a puck, and he knew another troublemaker when he saw one. The golden boy was not Fer's friend, even though she wanted him to be.

Time was strange in this place, and it hadn't touched Arenthiel. Behind his beautiful face, something else was looking out of those golden eyes—something rotten and twisted with long, long plotting and waiting. Arenthiel wasn't young. He was very, very old.

* * *

"What about the competition?" Fer asked Aren. She didn't want to talk anymore with him about clothes or glamorie; she wanted to know what tomorrow would bring.

Aren gave a graceful shrug. "All will be revealed, my

dear Gwynnefar." Then he dropped his voice, put his arm around her, and turned her away from the door, where Rook waited with Fray's hand gripping his shoulder. "Now, I have to warn you. That puck will want to make trouble between us for no other reason but that a puck's entire purpose in life is to make trouble." The corners of Aren's mouth drooped with mock-sadness. "If I can venture to guess, as soon as you step out of this room, young Robin will say something awful about me."

Knowing Rook, he probably would. But she kept quiet.

"If he does, will you just trust me that what he says is not true?" Aren asked.

She really, really needed a friend that she could trust. But she still wasn't sure about Aren. "I'll try," she said after a moment of hesitation.

"Good girl," Aren said, smiling his secretive smile. He pulled her to her feet and led her toward the door. "Now remember, do not wear the glamorie tomorrow."

Fer promised again that she wouldn't, then found herself outside Aren's door with Rook beside her and Fray looming behind them.

"Be careful of that one," Rook said in a low voice.

She glanced aside at him. Just as Aren had predicted. "You don't like him?"

He shook his shaggy head. "I don't, no. He's trouble, Fer."

She started walking. "You're trouble too, Rook."

He fell into step beside her. "I don't mean puck trouble." When she didn't answer, he went on. "Look, we like to stir things up, it's true. But we're not . . ." He shook his head. "Not like him. Pretty on the outside but something else on the inside."

"At least he's trying to be my friend," she said.

Rook stepped in front of her, his yellow eyes suddenly fierce. "You're wrong, *Lady Gwynnefar*. That creature is not what you think he is."

Fer studied Rook. For a second she saw him through Aren's eyes. Instead of a friend, she saw a surly, yellow-eyed puck, ragged and untrustworthy. Fray's words came back to her:

Pucks make trouble wherever they go.

And Grand-Jane's warning:

He is a puck, and that means it is his nature to be false, a liar and a trickster.

Fray and Grand-Jane—they were trying to protect her. And now Aren was too. Rook wasn't a human boy. He followed different rules, puck rules that she didn't understand. What if . . .

What if everybody else was right about Rook and she was wrong?

"Okay, Rook," she said. "Since we're talking about people who aren't what they seem, did you come with me to the nathe because you're my friend, or did you come here to cause trouble?" She put some of the Ladylike snap into her voice. "Tell me the truth!"

He took a step back as if she'd slapped him, his eyes wide. Then he turned fierce again. "You know what I am, Fer," he growled.

"Yes, I know what you are," she said, and turned away. He was a puck.

And maybe that was answer enough.

nine

In the very early morning, Fer went to be sure that Phouka and the rest of her bees were settled in the nathe's stables. She'd left the other bee behind to keep an eye on Rook. He wouldn't like that—he'd probably call it spying—but she'd taken responsibility for him, and she couldn't let him mess this up for her.

When she got back to her rooms, Rook had shifted into his dog shape and was crouched in a shadowed curve of the wall. As she came in the door, his fur bristled, and he growled.

"*Grrr* yourself, Rook," she muttered. He thought he looked so fierce, but in his dog-shape he had one ear that stood up and one that flopped over, and it made him look sort of funny. She looked more closely and saw that her bee was perched on the sticking-up ear. Clearly he hadn't noticed.

Leaving him to his growliness, she went into her room to get ready for her first encounter with the High Ones. Today the competition would begin, and she would have to prove herself worthy—in their eyes—to become the true Lady of the Summerlands. Her stomach jumped with nervousness. What would the contest be like? What would she have to do to win?

As soon as Twig had tied off the end of her braid, Fer examined herself in the room's long mirror. She wore her usual clothes and patched jacket. She looked like her own true self, just what Arenthiel had advised.

"You're ready," she told her reflection. Taking a deep breath, she paced into the main room.

Fray was ready too, burly and strong and dressed in wolf-guard gray. She stepped closer and bent to whisper into Fer's ear. "What about that puck, Lady?"

She eyed Rook. He was still a dog. Nice for him; it meant he couldn't talk, so he wouldn't have to answer any questions. "He'd better come with us," she whispered back. "So we can keep an eye on him."

A knock, and the door opened. The nathe-warden strode in. She looked Fer up and down, and Fer was sure she saw something in those green eyes. Was it scorn? "Gwynnefar," the warden said formally, "you are summoned to the nathewyr to prove your claim of Ladyship over the Summerlands. Come!"

* * *

In his dog shape, Rook trotted behind Fer and the idiot wolf-guard, following them through the twisty passages of the nathe. The warden led them to a grand double door inlaid in silver with a picture of some kind of flower. Fer had studied healing, and she knew about things like herbs and flowers; she'd know what it was. Rook glanced up at her. She looked nervous. *As she should be,* he thought.

The double doors swung open. Here it was, the nathewyr, a place that pucks had never been allowed to enter. This was where the High Ones showed themselves to their people, accepted their people's sworn oaths, and where they would pass their judgments. They'd brought Fer here to decide whether she could be the Lady of the Summerlands or not, which was stupid, since Fer was obviously a Lady and didn't need to win some competition to prove it.

He'd come here for another reason altogether. A puck reason.

The hall had several doorways in the walls—that was the first thing he noticed. Lots of ways out, then. Following Fer and the wolf-guard, he padded farther into the huge room. Along the walls were pillars made of living trees with silvery bark; they grew up from gnarled roots in the polished floor to twine their branches in a high, graceful ceiling. Glowing crystals hung from the tree-pillars' branches and sat in niches in the walls.

The nathewyr was crowded. A big hall like this, full of people as it was, should be echoey, but the silence pressed against his ears. To his dog-nose it smelled stuffy and old, just like the forest outside. Time didn't pass here, it just *was*.

Keeping their distance from him and Fer and the wolf-guard were Lords and Ladies of all kinds, some drooping like graceful flowers, others short and green-skinned like mossy stumps, or looming and hairy like broad bears, or blinking at him with wide deer eyes. Beautiful, all of them, with false glamorie, and shimmering with false power. As he passed, they snuck glances at him and Fer, and whispered to one another. Rook bared his fangs and grinned at them. At that, they exclaimed and drew away like salted snails.

Oh, would they be in for a shock, once he'd done what he'd come here to do.

Fer stopped and stood five steps ahead with her back to him, straight and slim in her patched jacket. None of the other Lords and Ladies had given her any sign of welcome; they'd only stared. The tips of her ears, Rook noticed, had turned pink. She must be able to hear the loud whispers—"false Lady" and "half human" and "bringing a nasty puck into our midst."

The crowd parted, and the golden Arenthiel creature glided up to Fer and bent over her, whispering. The fur on Rook's neck bristled. He watched as Fer turned to Arenthiel, eyes wide, and nodded. Arenthiel smiled, and Rook saw that even though his smile was beautiful, it was chill and sharp. Fer didn't have a puck's vision; she couldn't see it.

Arenthiel glanced aside at Rook and gave him a sly wink, as if they shared a secret. He knew that Rook's puck vision had seen him for what he truly was, Rook realized. He felt a growl grumbling in his chest.

But wait. He wasn't here to worry about Fer and her troubles. He was here to make trouble of his own. Trying to ignore Fer and the golden boy, he cast another look around the nathewyr, searching for the thing he'd come to find. There. At the end of the hall was a platform, and on it stood two carved wooden thrones. The High Ones' seats. The thrones were inlaid with silver that glinted faintly. Next to the thrones—there was the thing he'd come to find.

It rested on a pedestal, on a pillow made of deep blue velvet. A crown made of silver—silver oak leaves twined together with white gemstones shaped into acorns with silver caps, all shining with a cold, clear light. This was the prize that the High Ones would award to the winner of their competition, the new Lord or Lady of the Summerlands.

This was the thing his puck-brothers had sent him to the nathe to steal.

ten

The moment she stepped into the nathewyr, Fer knew she'd made a big mistake.

It was crowded, and every single Lord or Lady wore a glamorie. They were all so compellingly, glitteringly beautiful, it was like looking into the sun. Dazzled, she wanted to look away, at the floor or anywhere except at the people, but she kept her chin up and walked farther into the nathewyr.

As she passed, a tall bird-man with sharp black eyes and sleek, speckled feathers for hair wrinkled his nose as if he'd smelled something nasty. A graceful flower-maiden turned away, drooping. Others whispered and looked scornfully down their noses. Without a glamorie to hide her human side, Fer knew that to them she looked like a blot, a drab, plain thing. Not like a Lady at all.

Her ears burning, she found a place to stand, hardly aware of Fray at her side, or the dog-Rook a few steps behind her. Why hadn't Arenthiel told her it would be like this?

And there he was—Arenthiel glided up to her, looking just as gorgeously golden as he had the night before. "My dear girl!" he said, smiling. "You didn't wear your glamorie or finer clothes?"

"But—" she stammered. "You said—you made me promise not to wear the glamorie. You said my patch-jacket was right."

Arenthiel shook his head, mock-sorrowful. "Oh, dear me, no. You must have misunderstood. That is not what I meant, at all."

Fer's heart pounded. No, she hadn't misunderstood. He'd tricked her. She opened her mouth to ask him why, when the nathewyr fell suddenly silent. A cool, flower-scented breeze blew through the crowded room, and the doors swung open. The High Ones entered.

There were two of them, both women, tall and slender as birch trees, with dappled brown skin and hair as bright as braided sunlight. They wore white robes edged with silver and gold, and their feet were bare. The crowd parted and bowed like grasses in the wind as they paced slowly to the platform.

The High Ones were beautiful, of course—Fer had expected that. But they had power, too. She could feel it humming around her. Their power filled the nathewyr like water filling a cup, making the air thick and hard to breathe. As the High Ones settled gracefully onto their thrones, the weight of the room settled around them, as if they had grown roots down into their land. They had been here always; and they would always be here. They were ageless and terrible, wise and beautiful, all at the same time. Fer found herself bowing, just like all the others in the hall.

Except for Rook, she noticed, glancing back. He was standing on all four paws, gazing intently at something on the platform. She tried following his gaze, but she couldn't tell what he was looking at. Fray stood next to him; she'd keep him out of trouble, Fer knew.

One of the High Ones nodded, and a huge bear-man with bristly brown hair and a beard that grew all the way up to his close-set eyes stepped onto the platform. When he spoke, his deep voice filled the nathewyr. "The High Ones begin the contest." He pointed to a pedestal that stood next to the thrones. On it, a gleaming silver crown rested on a pillow. "The High Ones offer this crown. Whoever wins it also wins the power to rule the Summerlands as its Lord or Lady. Who would compete for this prize?"

Determined to be first, Fer started to step forward.

But another competitor beat her to it. "I will compete for the Summerlands crown!" shouted someone from behind her.

Fer whirled to look. A girl strode forward and bowed quickly toward the High Ones. She was taller and older than Fer. She didn't wear a glamorie, but she was beautiful anyway, dressed in silken finery, her black pants and long jacket studded with glittering rubies. She looked sturdy and strong; her skin was the color of charred paper; she had black eyes and wore her black hair in four long braids. Squinting, Fer could see smoldering orange coals at the tips of each of the girl's braids.

"I am Gnar of the Drylands," the girl announced in a crackling voice. "I am kin of the Lord there, and I seek to win a glamorie and a land of my own." She cast a keen look around the nathewyr. "No one here shall defeat me!"

On the platform, the High Ones nodded. The bearman nodded too. "Who else would compete for the crown?"

Fer stepped forward. "I do," she called out. She felt prickly as everyone in the nathewyr stared at her; she heard a faintly outraged "hmph!" from the Gnar girl.

"What is your name and your claim to the Summerlands, human?" the bear-man boomed.

"I'm Gwynnefar," she said, keeping her voice steady. "My mother was Laurelin, the Lady of the Summerlands, and I defeated the Mór, who killed my mother and father and tried to become the Lady in their place."

The High Ones stared down at her, their faces cold and blank. Were they even listening to her? If they ruled over all the lands, they must have known about the Mór and her evil. They hadn't done anything about it, though, had they? Maybe they didn't care.

"I . . ." Fer faltered. How could she convince them? "I feel a connection to the Summerlands and to the people who live there. I can open the Way between my land and the human world. And I have a crown that Leaf Woman gave me." The leafy crown, she meant. The wise and powerful Leaf Woman had crowned her with it after Fer had defeated the Mór. As she stated her reasons for being Lady, she felt the rightness of them. The High Ones had to see that she was the rightful Lady of the Summerlands.

Unless . . . unless they already had a reason *not* to see it.

On the platform, one of the High Ones whispered something to the bear-man.

"Yet, you are human," the bear-man said. "In all

time, no human has ever been a Lord or Lady of a land. And you do not wear your glamorie. Perhaps you are incapable of wearing it. How could you rule a land and its people without it, human girl?"

Fer nodded. So *that* was it. "Yes, I'm human. Half human. My father came from the human world. And yes, I have a glamorie, but I don't like wearing it. I don't trust it."

At that, the whispers broke out, filling the nathewyr with the sound of rustling leaves.

"The High Ones know that you have not taken oaths from the people of the Summerlands," the bear-man said.

"No, I haven't." Fer shook her head. "The deep-forest kin wanted to swear, and the other people do too, but I wouldn't let them. Taking oaths feels wrong to me."

At that, a few people exclaimed; the whispers grew louder. The bear-man raised a pawlike hand and a heavy silence fell. Then, "You do not wear the glamorie; you do not accept oaths. Are you all human, Gwynnefar, or are you one of us?"

Fer gulped. Oh no. Maybe they wouldn't even let her compete. "I am half human and I am one of you. I am both. And I *am* the true Lady of the Summerlands," she said firmly.

The High Ones leaned their heads together and whispered. One of them shook her head; the other one frowned and whispered something else. After a long moment, they nodded, agreed. "Hmmm," the bear-man growled. "You must prove yourself worthy, half-human, before the High Ones allow you to claim the Summerlands. That is their ruling. The High Ones will allow you to compete."

Fer released a relieved breath.

"Who else would compete for the crown?" the bear-man asked.

As Fer looked around, another competitor stepped forward, leaving puddled footprints behind him. He was tall and thin and greeny-pale all over, from the tips of his curly hair to his long, slender feet. Like Gnar, he didn't wear a glamorie, but his white satin suit was covered with tiny diamonds that glistened like dewdrops. He wavered into a deep bow. "I am Lich of the Damplands, kin of the Lady there. As is the way of our people since long before any"—he glanced aside at Fer—"humans came here, I will compete for the crown and become Lord of the Summerlands."

The bear-man nodded. "You may compete."

Fer frowned. They hadn't even questioned Gnar or this boy Lich. Was this even going to be a fair contest?

"Is there a fourth competitor?" the bear-man asked, gazing around the nathewyr.

Arenthiel stepped up beside Fer. She glanced aside at

him, and he gave her a wide, glittering smile. "Things are about to get interesting, dear girl," he said. In a louder voice, he announced, "I will compete for this prize!"

Fer stared. *What?*

Up on the platform, the High Ones were whispering again, and then they nodded and the bear-man was accepting Arenthiel as a competitor.

"Yes, Gwynnefar," Arenthiel murmured. "Long have I waited for the chance to claim a land of my own. At last my day has come. I am planning to become Lord of the Summerlands." His golden smile sharpened as he looked her up and down, seeing, she knew, her lack of glamorie, her ordinary clothes. "As you can see, I am already winning."

"You cheated," Fer protested.

He blinked, all innocence. "What a thing to say! I am no cheater. I only started the contest a bit early."

So he had. It had been a trick, him pretending to be her friend. She narrowed her eyes, but her glare bounced right off him. His smile glittered just as brightly. He ran a hand down the front of his embroidered coat, as if to say—*see how perfect I am?*

Around them, the nathewyr was emptying as the High Ones glided down from the platform, followed out of the hall by the Lords and Ladies. The other two competitors—the Gnar girl and the pale Lich boy—came to stand with Fer and Arenthiel, and the bear-man stepped down to join them.

Fer's knees felt shaky, standing there. The contest was beginning, and she was already losing. Oh, she had been stupid to believe Arenthiel's lies!

The bear-man surveyed them all, his furry face stern. "You may call me Lord Artos," he rumbled. "The contest begins later, this day. Your fitness to rule will be tested. You will ride, shoot bow and arrow, and demonstrate your mastery of the glamorie. Your strength will be tested. And"—and here Lord Artos turned his gaze on Fer—"also your weakness."

The girl named Gnar tossed her smoldering braids. "I will defeat you dull embers. I will win the crown and turn the Summerlands into a beautiful, dry land, with burning sand underfoot and no clouds in its ever-blue sky."

The tall Lich boy looked down his nose at her. "You will not, spark-thing. As the Lord of the Summerlands, I will bring to it coolth and peace and dripping fogs."

Arenthiel said nothing, but he smiled his perfect golden smile at all of them. He was confident, Fer could see. So sure he was going to win.

Inside her chest, Fer felt her heart turn into a hard

knot. Hard and determined. They wanted to turn the Summerlands into desert or swamp. Or—she eyed Arenthiel—into something worse. She was *not* going to lose her land and her people to any of them.

eleven

The contest would begin, Lord Artos had said, with a race. They would meet in the afternoon at the stables.

Fer arrived dripping wet, the first one there. She wiped rain off her face and leaned against Phouka's flank, looking out the stable's arched doorway. Outside, rain pounded down from low, lead-colored clouds. "It's going to be a wet ride," Fer murmured, and patted Phouka's neck. "Maybe muddy, too. Are you sure you don't mind running the race with me?"

As an answer, he whuffled his nose against her shoulder. He would do it, that meant.

"Thanks," she whispered, and took a deep breath, trying to calm herself.

After meeting the High Ones, Fer had only stopped

in her rooms for a few minutes, to eat a quick lunch and grab her backpack with its box of herbs in it. If Phouka got hurt in the race—or if she did—she might need the herbs for healing. She'd also left Rook in the rooms, watched over by Fray and Twig and one of her bees. He'd growled at her, clearly not liking it, but she had to make sure he didn't go out while she was gone and stir up trouble.

The stables were snug and dry and smelled of horse and—Fer eyed the nearby stalls—of other kinds of animals that could be ridden but were not horses. The stall at the end hid yet another mount. That stall had high walls, closing the mount inside, but Fer could hear bumps and thumps as the mount bashed itself against those walls. It sounded fierce, whatever it was.

She heard squishy footsteps; glancing out the doorway, she saw the tall boy, Lich, coming across the courtyard. He had his pale face turned up to the sky, letting the rain soak him from head to toe.

"Hi," Fer said as he entered.

Giving a damp sniff, he ignored her, then went into one of the other stalls. To Fer his mount looked a little like a horned goat, except that it had a fish's tail instead of back legs, and it was covered all over with glistening, mushroom-colored scales. Really, it was the perfect mount for a pouring-down-rain afternoon like this one.

The next to come in was Arenthiel. He wasn't wet at all—he had some magic that kept the rain off, Fer guessed, and that kept him looking perfect all the time, without a smudge or speck anywhere. He gave Fer one of his brilliant smiles as he stepped inside. "My dear Gwynnefar!" he said.

This time, Fer did the ignoring, busying herself by putting a few twists of braid into Phouka's mane, trying to keep her fingers from shaking. From the corner of her eyes, she watched as Arenthiel put a saddle and bridle on his mount, a golden horse with gleaming silver hoofs. As he led it out into the pouring rain, she realized that the horse was huge and powerfully muscled—so big, it made Phouka look like a shaggy pony in comparison.

Last to come was Gnar. Fer didn't recognize her at first; the girl from the Drylands was wrapped in a hooded cloak made of waxed canvas. As she entered the stable, Gnar threw back the hood, then stripped off the cloak and tossed it over a hay bale.

"Lovely day for frogs," she said dryly, with a glance at Lich and his goat-fish mount. After giving Fer a quick nod, she strode to the walled stall at the end of the stable; she opened its door and went in.

Fer stared, hearing more bumps and thumps. Curls of smoke leaked out from under the stall doors. What was *in* there?

The bear-man, Lord Artos, came in then, shaking drops of water from his furry head, clapping his huge hands together. "It is time," he rumbled. "Come." He led the way out into the rainy courtyard, where Arenthiel was waiting.

Fer put on her backpack and, gripping Phouka's mane, swung herself onto his back. Lich's mount trot-slithered ahead of her. Fer followed them into the middle of the courtyard. The rain poured down; in a few moments, Fer was soaked.

Last came Gnar and her mount. Fer stared. Gnar's mount was as big as Arenthiel's golden horse but shaped like a snaky lizard with clawed feet, coal-black scales, and a muzzle full of sharp teeth. Smoke drifted up from its red nostrils. It was wearing a canvas raincoat-like covering, just like Gnar's cloak, and it had a rain hat buckled over its head with two holes in it for its horns to stick out of. There were holes in the raincoat for wings, too, that the mount kept folded against its sides.

A big lizard with wings . . .

"Is that a *dragon*?" Fer asked.

A wide grin broke out across Gnar's dark face. Fer heard a *snrr-snrr* snorting sound—she was laughing! As Gnar laughed, puffs of smoke drifted up from her nose. Her dragon-mount stepped into the courtyard. Steam hissed wherever it set down its clawed feet.

The four competitors gathered around the bear-man. He had to speak loudly to be heard above the pouring rain. "You will begin the race here—" Lord Artos pointed toward the grassy area before the nathe. Through the rain, Fer could see that white tents had been set up and crowds of Lords and Ladies sheltered there, waiting for the race to begin. "You will take your mounts on the path through the forest and out to the Lake of All Ways. You will circle the lake twice, then return here."

Fer nodded. "Got that, Phouka?" she asked.

Phouka tossed his head and broke into a prancing trot, leading the other competitors across the puddled courtyard to the wide grassy lawn where the race would begin.

With the nathe looming behind them, the four of them lined up in the pouring rain: first Lich on his fish-goat; then Arenthiel and his huge horse, who were both perfectly dry, as if an invisible umbrella was open over them. Next to Fer rode Gnar and her dragon-mount. The dragon took high steps, as if it didn't like the feel of the wet grass beneath its claws. In the distance, thunder rumbled. Fer glanced aside at Gnar and caught her casting a nervous look at the sky. The rain came down harder, and Gnar hunched into her rain cloak.

She didn't like the rain, Fer realized. Well, that made sense; Gnar seemed to be made of smoke and flame. She couldn't be used to weather like this.

The High Ones had joined the Lords and Ladies under the tents.

"Be ready!" Lord Artos rumbled.

Fer gulped down a sudden surge of nervousness. She clutched Phouka's mane, ready for the race to begin.

"Be off!" the bear-man shouted.

Phouka leaped forward so suddenly that Fer almost lost her hold on his mane. She slid sideways, then gripped with her hands and with her legs and managed to stay on. Phouka pounded away from the nathe, heading for the dark forest on the other side of the wide lawn. Beside them raced Lich, his goat-mount stepping daintily with its front feet, its scaled tail swishing smoothly over the rain-wet grass. The golden horse ran easily, Arenthiel holding the reins with one hand, looking as if he wasn't even trying yet.

A crackly cackle from above, and Fer glanced up to see a dark shape pass overhead—Gnar and her dragon-mount. Flying! That was hardly fair.

But no. Nobody had said the mounts had to *run* the race. They just had to win it.

Fer crouched lower over Phouka's neck. They jolted over the grass, and then Fer found the rocking rhythm that made it feel as if Phouka was flying. They hurtled toward the forest. Ahead, Gnar's dragon-mount touched down on the grass; it took two running steps, then leaped into the air again, its wings rowing through the rain. Arenthiel's golden horse swerved in front of Fer, and a clod of mud kicked up by its heels hit her in the face. She ducked and scrubbed at the mud, and then they plunged into the dark forest.

The path was so narrow that they had to go one at a time. First went Gnar and her dragon, flying low under the tree branches—to stay dry, Fer figured. Then came Arenthiel. Fer saw a flash at his heels; he gave a sharp jab, and the golden horse leaped forward with a slash of blood-red across its side. Arenthiel was wearing spurs— sharp ones. The knot of determination in Fer's chest tightened. She and Phouka would *not* lose this race to somebody who would hurt his own horse to win.

Through the forest they raced, to the rooty gray wall, which opened like a curtain as they approached. As they burst out of the forest, the rain pelted down again. Ahead, the Lake of All Ways lay gray and flat under the lowering clouds.

"Twice around the lake," Fer shouted, reminding Phouka. He stretched out into a run, his hoofs skimming over the sodden grass. Fer wiped straggles of wet hair out of her eyes and peered ahead. Still in the lead, Gnar and her dragon faltered, as if the dragon's wings were being beaten down by the rain. It plunged to the ground, took a few staggering steps, and then flung itself back into the air, its wings flapping, Gnar crouched on its back, urging it onward. Just behind them came Arenthiel and his golden horse, running hard now. Fer saw more bloody slashes appear on the horse's sides. Lich pulled even with her and Phouka. His pale face was intent; his mount panted out steamy breaths, but it didn't slow.

The Lake of All Ways was wide, maybe a mile around, Fer guessed. Phouka ran steadily, but even pushing as hard as they could, Arenthiel's golden horse raced ahead of them. Fer held on and squinted to keep the rain out of her eyes. "*Faster*, Phouka," she urged. Phouka responded by surging until his nose was even with the golden horse's streaming tail. Right behind her, Fer could hear Lich's goat-mount.

Phouka snorted and put on another burst of speed and they drew even with Arenthiel. His big horse's strength was fading, Fer saw. It was too heavy for the wet course; it was struggling to slog along the muddy bank of the lake. Arenthiel glanced aside at her and slashed again with his sharpened spurs. The big horse slowed even more, and Fer and Phouka raced past them.

They could beat Arenthiel, she realized. She and Phouka went on, leaving Arenthiel and Lich farther and farther behind. They swept around the lake and started the second lap.

Suddenly Fer saw, way ahead, a dark shape plunge from the sky and crash next to the lake. Gnar's dragon. She and Phouka galloped closer. The dragon lurched to its clawed feet and stumbled on. Fer got closer, and then she and Phouka flashed past.

As they passed the dragon, Fer looked back over her shoulder, just in time to see the dragon crash to the ground again and Gnar tumble off its back. The fire-girl lay still, a heap on the ground.

"Phouka, wait," Fer shouted. Ignoring her, Phouka raced on. She jerked his mane to get his attention. "She fell off," she shouted. "She might be hurt."

Phouka slowed, then swerved, turning back to where Gnar and the dragon lay on the bank of the lake. They trotted up, Phouka blowing hard.

Gnar still wasn't moving; her dragon heaved itself away, its wings bedraggled, its raincoat slipping off. Flapping like a bird with a broken wing, the dragon headed for the drier forest path.

Quickly Fer swung off Phouka's back, her feet landing in squishy mud, and went to the other girl. Gnar's eyes were closed. Her skin was ashy gray, and she panted, wisps of fading smoke drifting from her mouth. She lay with her feet in the lake. Drops of rain speckled her face.

Fer gripped the shoulders of Gnar's raincoat and dragged her out of the water, then crouched next to her. With the back of her hand, she felt Gnar's forehead. The other girl's skin felt clammy and cool. Not the way a Drylands fire-girl should feel, Fer felt sure. She had some herbs that might help. She slung her knapsack to the ground and dug through it. Herbs for heating and drying, that's what she needed. Cayenne pepper would be best, but she didn't have any of that. Anise would work. And ginger. She had some of both, dried. With shaking hands, she found the paper envelopes with the herbs in them, crouching over to shelter them from the pouring rain.

Phouka, who had been standing nearby, snorted. Then she heard a heavy *clop-clop* of hoof-beats, and Arenthiel came splashing up, very tall on the back of his huge mount. He pulled the golden horse to a halt; it stood with its head lowered, snorting, bloody foam at its nostrils. They were both still completely dry, despite the rain falling all around them, and Arenthiel was absolutely clean, not a speck of mud on him.

"Aren," Fer called up. "I need your help! Can you use your magic to keep the rain off of Gnar?"

Arenthiel stared down at her. No smiles now; he looked grim and, somehow, older than he had before. "Why would I want to do something like that?" he asked, shouting to be heard above the rain.

"She's going to—" Fer glanced down at Gnar. The

fire-girl was shivering and flakes of ash coated her face. "The rain has damped her down to embers," Fer said. "She's going to go out—she's going to die."

"Oh, dear me. That would really be too bad," Arenthiel said with false sympathy. "Why don't you stay here and take care of her, Gwynnefar? I would help too, except that I have a race to win." Spurring his horse, he rode off, the rain parting like a silver curtain around him.

She stared after him. Aren was cold and cruel. How had she mistaken such a person for a friend, even for only a little while?

Fer turned back to her patient. That's what Gnar was, she realized. She wasn't going to leave her here to die just to win a race.

She had to get Gnar dry, somehow. Her patch-jacket might help; it had some of Grand-Jane's protective magic in it. She shrugged out of it, shivering as the rain soaked her shirt. With one arm she tried to hold the jacket over Gnar; with her other hand, she clumsily sorted herbs. Phouka edged closer, as if he was trying to help shield them from the wind and rain.

Lich came trotting through the rain on his fish-goat. Seeing Fer and Gnar, he stopped.

Fer looked up, blinking raindrops out of her eyes. "Lich, can you help?" she asked.

He was streaming with rain. He peered ahead, to where Arenthiel and his golden horse were stumbling away. If he went on, Fer knew, he might be able to catch Arenthiel and win the race.

"Her flame is going out," Fer told him.

With a steamy sigh, Lich slid off his fish-goat's back and squished over the grass to kneel on Gnar's other side. "She looks terrible," he said calmly.

She really did. "Just hold my jacket over her," Fer said, passing it to him. "Try to keep her dry."

Lich got to his feet and held the jacket over both of them.

It was a relief to not have the rain pounding down on her head and shoulders. Lich didn't seem to mind it at all. "Thanks," Fer called to him. Quickly she dumped dried ginger and anise into her hand. Oh, and she had some black pepper, too. She added all of it, mixing it with a finger. Gnar wouldn't want it in water, Fer guessed. She blew on her other hand to warm it up, then rested it on Gnar's forehead. The girl's eyes flickered open.

Fer bent closer. "Gnar, take this." She held her hand up to Gnar's mouth. "It'll help dry you out."

Gnar's mouth opened, and Fer tipped in the ginger, pepper, and anise.

A normal person would choke on such a spicy mixture, but Gnar swallowed, then coughed out a swirl of smoke and sparks. Her eyes popped open. She shoved Fer's hand away and struggled to sit up. "What are you—" She coughed again. "What are you doing?"

Fer shrugged and started stowing the packets of herbs in the knapsack. Phouka, curious as always, came closer and rested his nose on her shoulder. His wet mane dripped onto her neck. Brrr.

Tall Lich bent and peered under the jacket he still held. "You were down to embers and ash, Drylands girl," he said. "Gwynnefar helped you."

"She did?" Gnar turned to stare at Fer. "You did? Why?"

Fer blinked. "What do you mean, why?"

Gnar shook her head, as if Fer was being stupid. "You could have won the race. Why did you help me instead?"

"Because I had to," Fer tried to explain. Lich and Gnar looked at her blankly.

"It must be a human thing," Lich said.

"Must be," Gnar said. "Human or not, it was an extremely strange thing to do."

twelve

By the time Fer and Lich had found Gnar's dragon and gotten it, and Gnar, safely back to the nathe, the white tents had been taken down from the lawn. The rain had stopped, finally, but the sky was darkening, and a thick layer of mist surrounded the nathe. The High Ones had gone inside. The race was over, and Arenthiel had won.

They stumbled into the stable.

Arenthiel's horse stood shivering in its stall, its head lowered. It still wore its saddle and bridle, and it was soaking wet. Blood oozed from the slashes in its side. Arenthiel himself was not to be seen.

As Lich and Gnar cared for their mounts and then left, Fer led Phouka to his stall and used some wisps of straw to dry him, then gave him water and a bucket full of oats and draped a warm blanket over his back. "Thank you," she whispered to him. "I'm sorry we didn't win."

Phouka nickered and chewed his oats, watching with bright eyes as she went to Arenthiel's horse's stall. It twitched as she entered, but stood still as she took off its saddle and bridle, dumping them in the corner. She crouched and examined the slashes on its sides, made by Arenthiel's sharp spurs.

With a sigh, she got out her bags of herbs and bottles of tincture and made up a poultice, which she smeared on the slashes. More proof of Arenthiel's cruelty, that he could treat a horse so badly and then leave it chilled and bleeding, and without any food or water.

When she'd finished looking after the golden horse, she said goodnight to Phouka and headed back to her rooms. Time to look after herself. After such a hard race, she was tired down to her bones. She was soaking wet and had dried mud all over her face, and her braid was half unraveled. Every step up the stairs to the nathe hurt. Dinner. She'd have a dinner, and then a hot bath, and then a nice long sleep so she'd be ready for tomorrow.

At her own rooms, she opened the door; as she stepped inside, Fray and Twig pounced on her.

"Lady Gwynnefar!" Fray panted.

"Lady," Twig echoed, her eyes wide.

"It was just a short nap," Fray said. "I only slept for a moment."

"And then!" Twig put in, pointing at the door.

Fer closed her eyes, just for a second. She was *so* tired. She opened her eyes again. "And then what?"

"The puck!" Fray said. "He's snuck out. He's been gone for hours."

Fer leaned against the door. Oh no. This was just what she needed. What could Rook be up to now?

✳ ✳ ✳

In his person shape, Rook slipped through the dark tunnels of the nathe. He'd been slinking around for a while, staying out of the nathe-guards' way. Now it was growing late and the lights had been turned low, and nobody was about. Lucky for him. He had a crown to steal. Staying in the shadows, he made his way to the nathewyr, the big meeting hall.

Rook surveyed the room. It seemed bigger at night. Except for one or two crystals turned low, it was dark. The side doors, the ones he'd noticed this morning, were empty and unguarded. He felt a prickle of excitement under his skin. Once he'd gotten the crown, he could get out the doors and run for the forest in his horse form, and nobody would catch him.

He paced across the hall, the sound of his footsteps swallowed by the stuffy silence. He hopped up onto the platform and went over to the pedestal. The pillow was there, but the crown was missing. All he found was a circle inscribed in the velvet, where the crown had rested.

"Curse it," Rook muttered to himself, and flopped onto one of the High Ones' fancy thrones to think. With a fingernail he picked at the silver inlaid on the throne's arm. Hmm. They must put the crown away at night, for safekeeping. He'd have to try for it another time. But his brother-pucks had planned to meet him. He'd better go tell them he'd failed, so far, to steal the crown. That decided, he got to his feet and headed to one of the side doors, making his way out of the nathe.

The torches in the courtyard had been put out. The nathe-palace loomed behind him, dark except for a few windows watching like cats' eyes. The clouds from the day's rain were pulling away, leaving stars to hang low in the blue-black sky. Plenty of light for a puck. Rook slipped like a shadow down the gnarled steps and then popped his shifter-tooth into his mouth. As soon as his four paws hit the ground, he started to run, an easy lope that took him across the lawn and onto the path leading through the forest.

He ran on, silently, until he reached the outer wall, where he spat out the shifter-tooth and caught his breath.

Now this could get tricky. Shoving the tooth into the pocket of his ragged shorts, he paced to the wall, then tried the thing that Fer had done when they'd first arrived here, laying his hand against the twisted vines. For Fer, it had opened, but she'd been invited to come to the nathe, and she wasn't a puck. For him, the wall stayed closed.

"Nothing else for it, then," he whispered. Clinging to the woven vines with his fingers and toes, he climbed to the top of the wall. For a moment he paused there, looking back at the forest. No lights showed. He pricked his ears, listening. Nothing, not even a breeze in the treetops. Nobody out there tracking him, then.

Over he went, climbing down, then jumping onto the ground outside the nathe wall.

Off to his right, the Lake of All Ways glimmered in the starlight. Everything was silent and still.

Fer must have gotten back by now from her race to find him gone. He felt a twinge of something uncomfortable in his chest at that. Not *guilt*, was it? He was a puck! Pucks didn't feel guilt. Banishing the feeling, he sat down with his back against the vine-wall, waiting.

The grass was wet from the day's rain and not very comfortable, but after a while, his eyes grew heavy. It'd been a long night already, and he hadn't gotten much sleep the night before, either. To stay awake, he started counting stars.

✳ ✳ ✳

He woke up in the dark, flat on his back with some-body sitting on his chest, poking him. Somebody else was tickling his toes.

Nathe-wardens! was his first thought, and he struggled, and then he heard laughing. A heavy, dark shadow rolled off him, and he scrambled to his feet. "Asher?"

"I'm here, Pup," one of the shadows answered, and a light flared, a lantern. Its dim glow revealed Asher, and a grinning Tatter, and Rip, whose eyes gleamed red like embers in the darkness.

"Do you have it?" Asher asked. The crown, he meant.

"No," Rook answered. "Not yet."

"Huh," Asher said, and squatted down. "Tell us about it."

Rook sat on the damp grass, and they made a little circle with the lantern in the middle, Tatter to one side, Rip on the other, and Asher across from him. "It's just as you thought, Ash," Rook said. "They've got a silver crown for a prize. Whoever wins it is the new Lord or Lady of the Summerlands."

"All right," Asher said. He nodded, and the crystals braided into his long hair glinted in the lantern light. "Go on. When can you get it?"

Rook shrugged. "I'm not certain." He considered the possibilities. "They've got it locked up somewhere now. It depends on when I can get in, and when I can get away again. They've got guards watching us."

"Watching you and your friend Gwynnefar, you mean," Rip put in.

"No," Rook shot back. He didn't want to think about Fer, because this was a betrayal of trust he was plotting, right enough. "They're watching me, I meant."

Rip and Asher exchanged a glance at that. Asher drew back from the lantern light, and a shadow fell across his face. "At any rate, Rook, you're guarded," he went on. "When did that ever stop a puck?"

Rook forced a grin onto his face. "Not this time."

"Good," Asher said, and stood. "Stealing the Summerlands crown will be a wonderful trick, maybe the best puck-trick that ever was."

Rook nodded. It *was* a good trick. But . . . "Ash, there's one thing."

Asher raised his eyebrows, waiting.

"Fer—Lady Gwynnefar, I mean. To get me into the nathe she took responsibility for me."

"Ah!" Asher grinned. "Very clever of you, Pup. A perfect plan. That means she'll pay for any trouble you cause."

That's what it meant. But if it was such a perfectly pucklike plan, why did it make him feel sick and empty inside?

"This Gwynnefar Lady used her binding magic to

steal Phouka from us," Asher reminded him. "It's just what she deserves." He gave Rook a keen look. "Am I right, Pup?"

He knew that Asher was wrong. Fer hadn't bound anybody, and he didn't think she'd worked some kind of magic on Phouka. But he couldn't argue with his brothers, not now. Rook gave Asher a wooden nod. "You're right, yes."

Picking up the lantern, Tatter stood too, and so did Rip. They'd head through the Way now, back to the cave in the Foglands where they'd been hiding out with the rest of the pucks. A long way to come.

Rook got to his feet. "Once I've stolen the crown, I can bring it to you, if you like," he offered. That way he wouldn't have to see Fer's face when the puck-plot was discovered.

"Better not," Tatter answered.

Beside him, Asher shook his head. "The cave's not safe anymore. The Lord of the Foglands has taken notice of us. We'll have to move on soon."

Rook nodded. The pucks never got to settle anywhere for long. "So you'll come here again."

"That we will." Asher pulled out the bit of horn that he used to turn himself into a tall black goat with curling horns. Then he leaned closer to Rook to whisper in his ear. "Remember what you are, dear Pup. And remember what the High Ones and their Lords and Ladies are and what they do to the likes of us. She is one of them." Then he popped the shifter-horn into his mouth. Tatter and Rip shifted into dogs, and the three of them set off, racing over the glinting grass to the lake, where they could go through the Way.

Rook checked the sky. Off in the east it was stained with gray. Sunrise would come soon, which meant it was time to get back to the nathe.

Before starting up the vine-wall, he hesitated, rubbing the tiredness out of his eyes. Was he really going to do this? Betray Fer and let her take the blame for this puck-trouble?

He shook his head. The pucks were his brothers. They were his *home*. He had to stay true to them.

He climbed back up the vine-wall, and, as before, he stopped at the top to sniff the air and listen. All was dark and silent, but he had the prickly feeling of being watched. He waited for another moment, about to start down the other side, when he felt something *thunk* into the wall beside him, leaving behind a streak of pain on his leg.

An arrow!

Grasping the vines, he scrambled down the wall. As soon as he hit the ground, he started running. Lights flared on the path ahead, and he heard shouts. Abruptly he veered into the forest, dodging trees, pushing through thorny bushes. He flinched as another arrow sizzled past; he felt its fletchings brush his ear.

The nathe-wardens. They'd warned him before. If they caught him now, they'd kill him for sure.

From behind, he heard bushes thrashing and more shouts as the wardens followed him into the trees. He tripped on a root and went sprawling, and heard an arrow zip past, right where his head would have been. Curse it, they were good shots. He crawled into a bush, then flicked his shifter-tooth into his mouth. Four paws were faster than two feet.

More shouts, this time from behind and away to his left. They were trying to cut him off. Panting, he raced on, splashing through streams, squeezing past trees as the forest grew thicker, taking a route that would send him in a wide loop and then back toward the nathe-palace.

Finally he slowed, spat out the dog-tooth, and as he shifted, swung himself up into the boughs of a tree. Crouching there, he muffled his panting breath in his sleeve and listened for the sound of pursuit.

A rustling in the bushes right below him, and a nathe-warden paused, his head cocked, listening. His long knife glinted in the starlight.

Rook froze. If the warden looked up . . .

The warden listened for another moment; at a distant

shout, he raced away through the trees. The shouts of the other wardens faded.

Rook let out his breath. Now what?

The gray of dawn tinted half the sky. He could make his way back to the vine-wall, go through the Way, and tell his brother-pucks that he'd ruined their plan, almost getting caught.

Or he could go back to the nathe and trust that Fer would protect him from the nathe-wardens if they came after him there.

It'd be a risk. But it was worth it.

thirteen

"I said he was not to be trusted, Lady," Fray said from her post by the door.

"I know you did," Fer answered, turning at the wall and pacing back across the room. Her bee zipped around her head, as if it could feel her nervousness. She wore her nightgown and robe, but she hadn't been able to sleep. Rook wasn't back yet, and it had to be almost dawn.

Twig appeared at her bedroom door, rubbing her eyes. "What's the matter?"

"The puck's still gone. He's betrayed us," Fray said, her voice a low growl.

Had he? Had he *really*? Fer shook her head. "We don't know that he's done anything wrong."

"It's most likely," Fray said. "You don't know how

pucks truly are, Lady. That puck has tricked you. He can't be your friend; it's not in his nature."

A knocking, and they all turned toward the door. It swung open, and the stick-people came in with their loaded trays. "Breakfast," said the nathe-warden, a different one this time, a man who had wide brown eyes like a deer but who wore the same uniform as the other wardens she'd seen.

Fer stepped up to the door. "My friend has gone out," she said, thinking quickly. "He's under my protection. If he comes back, be sure to let him in, all right?"

The warden blinked his big eyes, then bowed. "As you command."

The stick-people set down their trays and left again, and the door closed behind them. Fray and Twig started to eat, and Fer sat on a cushion at the low table and poured tea and tried to eat something, but worry gnawed at her stomach. What would the nathe-wardens do to Rook if they caught him? What would they do to *her*?

The next part of the competition was this morning. It would be shooting with bow and arrow, the bear-man had told them yesterday, and after losing so badly in the race, she had to win. She knew how to shoot. The Mór had taught her, and she had practiced until she was good at it. But if Rook was out there causing some kind of trouble, the High Ones might not let her compete at all.

She was tearing pieces off a sweet roll when the door burst open. "Your friend has returned," said the warden blandly, and shoved Rook into the room. The warden left, slamming the door behind him.

Rook panted as if he'd been running, his black hair was a mass of tangles, and he had a long, bloody scratch on his leg.

Fer dropped the roll and set down her teacup with a clatter. "Rook!" She jumped to her feet. "Are you all right?"

"I am, yes," Rook answered, catching his breath. His eyes went to the table. "Is that breakfast?"

Not for the first time in their friendship, she wanted to strangle him. "Where have you been?" she asked. He opened his mouth to answer, and she interrupted. "And don't say 'none of your business.' It *is* my business. If you get into trouble, then I get into trouble." She waited for him to explain himself, but he didn't speak, just stood scowling at the floor. Okay. Fine. She still had plenty of healing herbs in her box. "I'll put some medicine on that scrape so it doesn't get infected."

"It's all right," he said, his voice rough, and brushed past her to the table, where he crouched and tore into the food like a ravenous dog.

No more *Oh, Rook*. She was starting to get mad. She spun on her heel and stalked into her room to get ready.

When she had dressed—her jeans and patch-jacket were still a little damp from the day before—and Twig had finished braiding her hair, Fer picked up her bow and slung the quiver of arrows over her shoulder and went back into the main room. The bee was on the table, leaving tiny footprints in the butter from breakfast. Rook was sprawled awkwardly across two of the pillows, sound asleep.

She stood looking down at him. Rook was ragged and grubby, and he was, for sure, keeping dark secrets from her. "You were right, Fray," she admitted. "I shouldn't have let him come with us,"

"It's all right, Lady," Fray said gruffly from over by the door. "I'll keep a closer eye on him. He won't slip away again, not if I can help it."

After Fer had checked on Phouka, she headed out to the green lawn before the nathe, where the archery contest was set to begin. Like the day before, tents had been set up, but now they were there to protect the Lords and Ladies and the High Ones from the sun, which blazed down from a brilliant blue-glass sky.

As she stepped out onto the lawn, gripping her bow, Lord Artos loomed up before her.

"Gwynnefar," he rumbled. "The High Ones wish

to speak with you before this morning's competition begins."

Fer felt a twist of worry in her chest. "Okay," she answered, and followed Artos to the tent. The air beneath it was cool and shadowed. The two High Ones, dressed in white, their braided sunlight hair like crowns on their heads, sat apart from the other Lords and Ladies. Artos led her to them and then stepped aside, leaving Fer standing on the grass before them.

For a long moment, the two High Ones looked her over, and Fer felt the heaviness of their gazes. Their power was rooted so deeply; it made her shiver, standing this close.

"Gwynnefar," one of them said, and Fer almost jumped, the voice was so unexpected. It was cool and clear, like water flowing over smooth rocks.

She wasn't sure what she was supposed to do. Bow, maybe? Kneel? Part of her wanted to kneel before such power. But she didn't; she just tried to stand straighter.

"We ask you, Gwynnefar," the other High One said. "Are you content with the outcome of yesterday's contest?"

"Not really," Fer answered.

"But you saved your fellow competitor's life," the High One said smoothly. "Does that not content you?"

"Well, yes. It does," Fer said. "But I lost the race."

The dappled faces of the High Ones were calm, and they didn't speak, they just looked. Their power rippled around her. Fer felt like squirming under their gazes, but kept herself still. It felt as though they were seeing into her deepest, most secret heart.

What did they see there?

"What is it to win?" asked the first High One at last.

"And what is it to lose?" asked the other, in a lower voice.

Fer blinked. What did *that* mean?

"That is all," Lord Artos said, suddenly appearing at her shoulder.

Fer felt the High Ones watching her as she left the tent.

What had they wanted with her? Were they glad that she'd lost? Or did they mean something else?

Leaving the cool tent, Fer broke out in a sweat just crossing the grass. As she reached the others, she took off her patch-jacket and tied it around her waist, then put the quiver back over her shoulder again.

"Hi," she said to Lich and Gnar.

The Drylands girl gave her a wide grin in return. "Good morning, Strange One." Then she tilted her face toward the sky as if she was drinking in the sun's warmth.

Beside Gnar stood Lich. He carried a bow as tall as he was. On his head he wore a wide hat, keeping his pale face shaded from the sun. "Lovely day for lizards," he said, with a dour look at Gnar.

"You're all right?" Fer asked Gnar. She certainly looked healthy.

"Better than all right," Gnar answered, holding up her bow. It was black, of course, and its ends were carved with dragon heads that had glittering red jewels for eyes. "I am an excellent archer, and I am planning to win today."

Fer found herself smiling at the other girl's fiery confidence. "Not if I can help it," she said, holding up her own bow.

Gnar gave her *snrr snrr* laugh, smoke drifting up from her nostrils.

Still smiling, Fer busied herself buckling on a leather bracer so the bowstring wouldn't take the skin off her left forearm, then looked around. A row of white targets with black bullseyes had been set up way across the lawn, at the edge of the forest. Hmm. Somehow she felt sure that this part of the contest would be more challenging than just shooting at targets.

Arenthiel came bounding across the grass to join them, flashing his glittering smile. "Good morning, all," he said brightly, as if he hadn't refused to help Gnar the day before; as if he hadn't left his horse cold and bleeding it its stall.

In silent agreement, Fer, Lich, and Gnar turned away, ignoring him.

Then Fer had a thought and turned back. She knew why Gnar and Lich wanted to win the silver crown. They each wanted to turn the Summerlands into a home—into a desert, for Gnar, or into a swamp, for Lich. "Arenthiel," she asked. "Why do you want to be Lord of the Summerlands?"

He raised his perfect eyebrows. "It is a wild and ugly land," he said smoothly. "As its Lord, I will tame it. I will make it beautiful."

But her Summerlands were already beautiful. What Arenthiel really wanted, she suspected, was to control the land. His idea of beauty, she guessed, would be to cut down the forests and divide the Summerlands into squares and rectangles of neatly trimmed lawn.

She *was not* going to let that happen. He had won the race the day before, but today she would win.

Over by the tents, Lord Artos, the bear-man, was speaking with the High Ones. He bowed and crossed the lawn to where the contestants waited. "The archery contest will begin in a moment. You will shoot there—" He pointed at the targets at the edge of the forest. "And there." Then he pointed behind them.

Fer turned with the others to look and saw that another row of four targets had been set up on the edge of the grass closest to the nathe. Maybe a quarter of a mile of lawn lay between the two sets of targets.

"Your skill with the bow will be tested," Lord Artos went on, "your accuracy, the speed at which you loose a shot, and your stamina. The first round begins here." He nodded at the targets nearest the nathe. "After each round, I will tell you what comes next."

"That seems simple enough," Arenthiel said, all cool confidence. Over his shoulder he carried a crossbow inlaid with silver. Its shape, with the bow at the end and the long stock, reminded Fer of a dragonfly.

Lich was busy getting ready, pulling his longbow back against his leg to string it, then adjusting his wide-brimmed hat. He wore a long-sleeved shirt, Fer noticed, and long pants, both made of white leather. Hot, she figured, but it protected him from the sun. Lich saw Fer watching him and pointed with his chin at Arenthiel, who was using what looked like a crank to pull back the string of his crossbow. "He's not an archer," Lich said, in a low voice.

Gnar was listening too, and stepped closer. "Crossbow," she said, as if that explained it.

"What do you mean?" Fer asked.

"He shoots a crossbow," Lich said calmly. "It requires less skill, and far less practice to become accurate. But he will be slow to reload."

"It'll be heavy, too," Gnar added, with one of her flashing grins. "Though so is that tree you've got there." She pointed at Lich's longbow.

Lich gave a damp sniff, but Fer was sure she saw a smile in his eyes. Fer couldn't help smiling herself. Lich and Gnar were her competition, but she was starting to like them.

"Are you ready?" Lord Artos's rumbling voice interrupted. He led them over to the four targets—one for each of them. The white canvas they were made of glittered under the hot sun. Nearby were the tents where the Lords and Ladies and the High Ones sat in shady comfort, watching.

"The first round tests your accuracy. From twenty paces, you will each take five shots. Begin!"

Fer felt a sudden jolt of excitement. But no. To shoot cleanly, she had to have steady hands. She took a deep breath and ran her fingers along the smooth curve of her bow.

She knew how to shoot. She'd practiced every day she'd spent back in the human world with Grand-Jane. The tips of the three fingers she used to draw back the bowstring were callused and her arm muscles were strong. Carefully she shut out the tent full of spectators, and the heavy gaze of the High Ones, and the sun blazing down on the top of her head, and the other archers. It was just her and the target. She reached back and took an arrow out of the quiver and fitted it to the string. Pulling back the string to her cheek, she sighted down the arrow to the center of the target. She waited one breath, two, then felt the rightness of the shot settle in, and released the string. Her arrow flew cleanly and landed with a satisfying *thunk* on the inner edge of the bullseye.

Without hurrying, she shot four more times, hitting the black twice more, and not far off it on the other two shots. When she looked up, the others had finished.

Gnar had done about as well as Fer had, though smoke drifted up from the feathered ends of two of her arrows.

All of Aren's arrows were in the black.

And Lich's five long arrows were clustered in a tight circle at the center of the bullseye. Perfect shooting.

All right. Fer took a deep breath. She would just have to shoot better.

"Next round!" Lord Artos bellowed, clapping his heavy hands. "At speed, collect your arrows. Run to the other targets. Take five shots. Leave the arrows in the target. Run back." He clapped again. "Be off!"

Right! Fer dashed to the target and jerked out her arrows. Jamming them into the quiver and clutching her bow, she set out across the lawn to the other targets. Gnar passed her, laughing, and Fer put on a burst of speed to keep up. They raced together to the targets near the forest.

Panting and wiping sweat out of her eyes, Fer stepped up to the line marking her distance from the target. As quickly as she could, she fired off five arrows. Gnar had already finished, she noted, and was speeding across the lawn, but her arrows had barely hit their target. As Fer spun to head back, she saw that Arenthiel was frantically cranking back the string of his crossbow, still only on his third arrow. Hah! Gnar had been right about the slower crossbow.

Lich had finished shooting too—perfect again, Fer noted with dismay—and had headed back across the lawn. He ran slowly, though, and his path wavered, as if he'd lost sight of where he was going. Fer raced past him.

At the other end, Gnar was already shooting. One of her arrows thunked into the bullseye and burst into flame.

"Five more shots," Lord Artos told Fer. "Then collect the arrows and take them to the other targets to shoot, as before."

This was more like a foot race than an archery contest, Fer realized. Blinking sweat out of her eyes, she fired off her five shots and collected her arrows.

Lich, she noticed, was just starting his round. He'd taken an awfully long time getting across from the other targets. Under his hat, his face was bright red, and he was panting out gusts of steam.

"Are you okay?" Fer asked as she hurried past him.

He didn't answer.

She raced across the wide stretch of grass to the targets near the forest. The sun blazed down; she panted and wished for some cool water. This time when she lined up to shoot, her legs were shaking, and her fingers were slippery with sweat. She wiped them on her jeans and closed her eyes for a second. Calm. Cool.

Okay, ready. She opened her eyes again. As she pulled out an arrow, Lich staggered up. With a clatter, his quiver dropped to the ground and the arrows scattered. He dropped to his knees to pick them up.

Fer started to sight on her target, then stopped. "Lich," she asked again. "Are you all right?" If she had to, she'd ask it a third time to get him to answer.

He kept his head lowered. The arrows fell from his limp hand.

He was *not* okay. Fer set down her bow and arrows and went to him. As she reached out to steady his shoulder, he tipped over onto the grass. Fer knelt by his side. Lich's face was even redder now, but blotched with pale spots. His lips were pale too, and cracked. "Oh no," Fer whispered. He was used to chilly, wet weather. This archery race might kill him if he didn't get cooled off.

Fer looked up. Gnar had just finished shooting, and was busy pulling her smoking arrows out of the target. "Gnar!" Fer shouted.

The fire-girl stuffed her last arrow into her quiver and strode over. She glanced curiously down at Lich. "What is it, Strange One?"

Fer took Lich's hat off and held it over his face to shade him from the blazing sun. It was pretty obvious what was happening. "He's heat sick," Fer said impatiently. She hadn't brought her knapsack with her this time, so she couldn't use herbs to heal him. The forest. It was shady there. But Lich was too heavy to move by herself. "We need to get him under the trees, where it's cooler. Will you help?"

Gnar tossed one of her smoldering braids over her shoulder. "It's another odd thing to ask, Strange One, but I'll do it."

As she spoke, Arenthiel trotted up, panting. Ignoring Fer and Gnar, and Lich sprawled on the ground, he started cranking back the string of his crossbow.

He could help too, Fer realized. He probably wouldn't, but she had to ask. "Arenthiel," she called. "Lich needs water, as soon as possible. Will you run back and fetch some from the nathe?"

"Fetch?" Arenthiel asked, turning his back on them and taking up a shooting stance. "I do not *fetch*." He glanced over his shoulder at them and gave a smug smile. Then he turned and fired off an arrow at the target.

Fer gripped Lich's shoulder. "Come on," she said to Gnar. "You take that side."

Together, they dragged Lich across the grass, out of the blazing sun and under the shadowed eaves of the forest. Kneeling by his side, Fer fanned his face with his hat.

His eyes, which already looked sunken, flicked open. "I believe I may dry," he whispered.

"You'd better not," Gnar threatened. She nodded at Fer. "I'm faster than you are. I'll do the fetching."

Gnar left, and Fer kept fanning. If only she had her box of herbs! For cooling she could use mint or mallow. Even better would be . . . She looked up. Here among the weeds at the edge of the forest—she might find borage growing. It was a common enough herb. "I'll be right back," she said to Lich, and scrambled to her feet.

Grand-Jane had taught her that borage was also called bees-bread and that a good way to find it was to watch where bees were gathering. A scrubby patch of weeds lay not too far off, and it was humming with bees, busy in the hot sunlight. Fer ran over, looking among the grasses and weeds for borage's distinctive star-shaped blue flowers. There! She wasn't wearing gloves, so the prickly hairs on the leaves and stems stung her fingers. "Ow, ow, ow," she muttered, pulling up two of the borage plants and hurrying back to Lich. Trying to ignore the stings, she broke open the stems. "Here you go," she murmured to Lich, and smeared the sap from inside the borage plant on his face.

"Ohhhh," he sighed. "Better."

Good. His skin was already less red and blotchy. Fer rubbed more cooling borage sap on his neck, and on the inside of his wrists. Then she picked up his hat and started fanning again. She gazed back toward the nathe, at the other targets and the white tents. The High Ones and Lords and Ladies were leaving, she saw. The bear-man was taking down the targets.

The archery contest was over, and Arenthiel had won. Again.

fourteen

A note arrived in Fer's rooms. The contestants would have the rest of the afternoon to recover, Lord Artos informed her, and in the evening, they would meet in the nathewyr for the final part of the competition. There, they would each demonstrate their mastery of the glamorie.

Something else was written at the bottom of the note from the bear-man, an extra note for her, written in different handwriting.

Remember, Gwynnefar, the note said. *The contest is a test.*

"Oh, I bet I know who wrote that," Fer muttered to herself. It sounded like one of the High Ones' completely confusing statements. Winning was losing, contests were tests. What were they up to, exactly?

Fer shook her head, setting aside her confusion. She had other things to worry about now.

The next part of the contest was going to be a problem.

Fer didn't like the glamorie. Having it on made her feel cold and calculating. It made her feel not very much like her own self. It was hard to believe that her own mother had worn it, but she must have—she'd been a Lady, after all. So Fer would wear it too, just for today.

After having a rest in her room, she washed her face, pulled off her jeans, T-shirt, and patch-jacket, and put on the clothes she'd found in the chest back in her little house in the Lady Tree. Her mother's clothes—the slithery-smooth silk shirt, the trousers and boots, the vest embroidered with oak leaves. Then she laid out her mother's soft, knee-length green coat on the bed next to her patch-jacket. Which one should she wear? The fine coat matched the glamorie, but Grand-Jane had stitched protective spells and herbs into the jacket. She gnawed on her thumbnail, considering.

Then she nodded. Just for this evening, she would be a Lady, through and through. She picked up her mother's coat and put it on over the vest. Then Twig combed her hair and braided it.

"Now this," Twig said, setting on Fer's head the

crown of undying oak leaves. "And this." She handed Fer the wooden box with the glamorie in it.

Taking a deep breath, Fer reached inside and pulled out the shimmering web of the glamorie. A flick of the wrist and she tossed it over herself, shivering as it clung to her hair, her face, her arms. As it set its chilly hooks into her skin, Fer shuddered, and then, as the glamorie took effect, she felt the nervousness about the next part of the competition fall away.

"There," breathed Twig, crouching and gazing up at Fer. "You're a Lady. Head to toe, you are."

Yes. She was. Fer felt the high collar of the shirt brush her chin, so she gave a proud tilt to her head and went out to the main room.

Rook, his usual barefoot, grubby self, was still asleep on the pillows. Her bee rested on his elbow.

"Wake up the puck," she found herself saying to Fray.

Wide-eyed, Fray bowed. "Yes, Lady Gwynnefar," she whispered.

Fer shook her head. Her voice had sounded so cold, and Fray seemed so awed, and Twig had crouched on the floor, so worshipful. She rubbed her arms, chilled. The glamorie affected them so strongly. Maybe it was affecting her too.

It was only for tonight, she promised herself. Despite

what the High Ones had said, she knew she'd lost the first two parts of the competition. Tonight she had to wear the glamorie—she had to win.

✳ ✳ ✳

Somebody kicked the bottom of his foot, and Rook bolted upright, suddenly awake. The wolf-girl glared down at him. "Get up, Puck," she growled.

"Go bite somebody else, you stupid wolf," Rook growled back.

She reached down to grab him, and he skittered away. Then he realized that one of Fer's bees had attached itself to the sleeve of his shirt. "Get off," he said, brushing at it.

Wolves, bees, bad dreams. Not the best way to wake up.

Fer stood by the open door, watching. She looked stern, and not very friendly. She was wearing the glamorie; he could see that clearly enough. "What's going on?" he asked.

"We are going to the nathewyr for the last part of the competition," Fer said.

"Go ahead," Rook said with a shrug.

The wolf-guard's hand came down on his shoulder. "You're coming with us, Puck."

"I'm not, no," he said, pulling away. He had his own plan—to steal the silver crown—and it'd be better for Fer if he wasn't with her when he carried it out.

142

"You are, *yes*," Fer said icily. "I don't like the glamorie, but it helps me think more clearly, at least. It's obvious that you're up to something, Rook. I'm not leaving you here unguarded." She nodded at the wolf-guard. "Bring him."

The wolf kept a grip on his arm, dragging him out the door and down the stairs after Fer, who stalked away, her braid ticking back and forth.

Oh, the glamorie had its hooks in her. "Wearing that thing is like wearing a lie," he called to her as they came out into the polished hallway.

She stopped and whirled to face him. "Oh, *lies*. You know all about lies, don't you, Rook? Where did you go last night? Hmm? Are you going to tell me the truth about that?"

No. He couldn't.

She stepped closer. "I really, really wanted to trust you," she whispered, and it was Fer talking, not the glamorie. "I needed you to be my friend."

He stared down at her, feeling that strange tugging at his heart again. He closed his eyes, concentrating. Even though they were on the outs, the thread had started to spin itself out again, connecting him to her. A *binding spell*, his puck-brothers had called it, but that wasn't what it was. Grimly he snapped it, and opened his eyes again. "Fer," he warned, "don't forget that I'm a puck."

143

She turned away again. "How could I forget that?" she called over her shoulder. "You won't ever let me forget." She paced ahead of him down a hallway crowded with other Lords and Ladies and their retinues, who all turned to stare as they passed.

Still gripping his arm, the wolf-guard dragged him after her. "You don't have to hold on to me so tightly," Rook complained.

She ignored him.

＊ ＊ ＊

Fer felt the eyes of all the other Lords and Ladies fix on her as she entered the nathewyr, followed by Rook and Fray. The argument with Rook had made her feel achy and sad, and entering the hall made all her worry about the competition boil up inside her, but then the glamorie sparkled over her skin and made her feel taller, more noble, and not nervous or sad at all.

Keeping her chin high, she paced to a spot before the platform, joining Lich and Gnar. The other two competitors had been given glamories to wear for this part of the contest. Their glamories were so fine, they practically glowed, Lich with the pearly light of the moon reflected on water, and Gnar with sparks of keenest flame. They both looked as if wearing the glamorie was the most natural thing in the world. Gnar gave Fer a preening smile, as if to say, *Yes, I know I am beautiful.*

On the platform, the High Ones' thrones were empty. The prize Fer had come to win—the Summerlands crown—was covered with a midnight-blue velvet cloth and rested on its pedestal beside the thrones. The Lords and Ladies in the nathewyr waited, whispering to one another, filling the room with a sound like rustling leaves.

As Fer joined them, Gnar grinned and Lich gave her a solemn bow. "I thank you, Gwynnefar," he said in his calm voice, "for helping me this morning."

"I helped too," Gnar interrupted.

Lich turned his cool gaze on her. "By the time you brought the water, it had all but boiled away. If not for Gwynnefar, I would have dried."

The quick grin flickered over Gnar's face. "True enough!" She looked Fer up and down. "You're wearing a crown." She leaned forward to see better, and Fer felt the heat of the other girl's skin, like being close to a hot stove. "Are those real leaves?" Gnar asked.

Fer nodded. "It was given to me when I helped free the Summerlands from the Mór."

"But that one is the real Summerlands crown," Gnar said, and pointed at the pedestal where the covered crown rested.

Maybe. Her plain leafy crown felt more right for her land than a heavy silver one. To change the subject, Fer said, "Your glamorie is very beautiful." Gnar liked compliments, she knew.

Gnar gave her preening smile again and flicked sparks from the tips of her fingers. "Beautiful, yes. But I suppose, Strange One, that even you know what the glamorie is really for."

She thought she did. But she wasn't sure.

"Yes," Arenthiel put in from behind her. Fer, Lich, and Gnar didn't acknowledge him, but he stepped up beside them anyway, bestowing upon them his superior smile. "A Lord or Lady wears the glamorie in order to rule."

And there it was. *Rule.* It meant the Lady, alone, had all the power in her land, and it meant that her people had no choice in what they did—if she ordered something, they had to obey. The glamorie gave its wearer beauty, and it gave her power. And, Fer was starting to suspect, the glamorie changed its wearer too—it made her cold and calculating and uncaring. As an answer, Fer's glamorie gave a chilling sparkle. To rule was right, the glamorie meant.

No. It was *not* right. Fer felt a core of stubbornness forming inside her. A core that the glamorie chilling her skin couldn't touch. Her land was wild and free and wonderful. It could not be tamed or cut into neat rectangles—it would not be ruled, and neither would its people. "Even though I'm wearing the glamorie now," Fer said steadily, "I won't be that kind of Lady."

"What do you mean?" Gnar asked, no longer smiling.

Fer spoke more loudly, into a growing silence. "To use the glamorie to rule is wrong." Her voice rang out in the hall; all the Lords and Ladies had heard. They stared, as if stunned by her words.

Lich and Gnar stared at her too. "See?" Gnar whispered. "Strange."

"Strange indeed," Arenthiel put in. He nodded at Rook, where he stood with the wolf-guard's hand on his shoulder. "She brings a puck into our midst, and she is a bit of a puck herself, isn't she, Lich? Isn't she, Gnar?"

"She is," Gnar said, taking a step back, as if Fer had suddenly contracted some horrible disease. Lich wrinkled his nose with disgust.

"Well, Gwynnefar?" Aren persisted. "You do claim friendship among the pucks, do you not?"

Did she? She was mad at Rook, but it didn't mean she wasn't friends with him anymore. Fer glanced over her shoulder at Rook. He met her gaze and looked away, as if he was feeling guilty about something.

Aren smiled his false, glittery smile. "You do know about pucks, don't you, Gwynnefar? Pucks are a force of chaos. They are wild. Ungoverned by any rule. Dangerous. They upset everything. Like all those who live in these lands, the people of the Summerlands have a bit of wildness in them. Wolf-people. Fox-people. Deer-people. Badger-people. Am I right?"

Fer nodded.

Aren went on. "Without a glamorie, worn by a proper Lady, without sworn oaths, the people of the Summerlands have no *rule*. They will become like the pucks; they will become wild. And you seem to desire this. I expect you would call it *freedom*, or some such foolish thing. Truly, I think you are dangerous as well."

Wait. She didn't like the idea of rule, but it didn't mean . . . She shook her head. "I'm not dangerous," Fer protested. She looked to Gnar and Lich for help, but they backed farther away. Maybe their glamories were making them think cold, unfriendly thoughts. No help there.

Aren stepped closer and whispered, so only she could hear. "I am beginning to think, my dear girl, that perhaps you are more dangerous than you realize."

fifteen

Rook tried to shrug Fray's hand off his shoulder, but the wolf-girl was taking her duties very seriously. It wouldn't be easy to slip away, vigilant as she was. He watched as Fer stood talking with the other contestants.

Then Fer said loudly something about how using the glamorie to rule was wrong. Oh, the fancy ones in the nathewyr didn't like that. Rook could hear them exclaiming to each other, disapproving of Fer and her bid to become a Lady like them. Or, maybe, not like them at all.

The false one, Arenthiel, said something to her, and she glanced over at him.

Instead of meeting her eyes, he stared at the floor. He

had a crown to steal. He couldn't afford to think about Fer right now.

After a short while, the double doors at the end of the nathewyr swung open, and the High Ones paced in. Everybody in the hall bowed.

Everybody except him, that is. He watched the High Ones carefully. He could feel their power, the way the nathewyr changed when they entered it, but their power couldn't command *him*.

The big bear-man stepped onto the platform and bowed. Again the gathered Lords and Ladies bowed.

Rook snorted. Stupid High Ones and their stupid formality.

The wolf-guard's grip tightened. "Steady on there, Puck," she grumbled.

The bear-man surveyed the hall, then began to speak about the results of the race and the archery contest, and explained how the contestants' mastery of the glamorie would be tested.

As he spoke, Rook eyed the pedestal, where the crown was covered with a cloth. If he waited to steal the crown until Fer's glamorie was tested, all eyes in the nathewyr would be on her. Even the wolf-guard Fray would be distracted. A perfect moment to slip out of her grip and grab the crown. In his four-legged dog shape he could run to an unguarded doorway, through the nathe, and out to the courtyard. Once there he could shift into his horse form. After that, nobody would catch him.

Then he had a thought that made him feel hollow inside. After stealing the crown, he'd never see Fer again.

He shook his head, trying to shake that thought away. He was not bound to Fer. A puck and a Lady could *never* be friends. He just had to stop thinking about how she'd look when she found out he'd betrayed her.

But he couldn't. He stood with his head lowered, thinking. What if . . .

What if he didn't steal the crown after all? He could explain to his brothers, and they would understand. Wouldn't they?

Rook glanced aside and realized that Arenthiel was standing right next to him. "Hello, Dog," he murmured, his false smile fixed on his face.

"Grrrr." Rook bared his teeth.

Arenthiel leaned closer. "You, young puck, are about to be very useful to me."

What?

On the platform, the bear-man was pointing at the cloth-covered crown.

"Ah," Arenthiel whispered. "It's time."

Rook felt his hackles going up. Time for what? Something about this smelled bad.

Arenthiel gave him a brisk nod, then whirled and

paced past Fer and the other contestants and leaped onto the platform, striding past the bear-man and the High Ones to the pedestal where the cloth-covered crown rested.

Rook strained to see better.

Arenthiel reached out and lifted the cloth from the crown. Then he staggered dramatically back, his eyes wide. "My Lords, my Ladies!" he cried. He lifted the thing resting on the pillow and held it up so everyone in the nathewyr could see. "This is not the Summerlands crown!"

No, it wasn't. It was a crude circular thing made out of twigs and dried mud.

"The true Summerlands crown has been stolen!" Arenthiel announced.

The hall erupted in a babble of voices; the High Ones rose to their feet.

Rook stared, astonished. Somebody had gotten to the crown before he could steal it for his brother-pucks. But who?

Arenthiel dropped the mud crown onto the pedestal as if it was a poisonous snake, then strode to the edge of the platform. "Who would do such an abominable thing?" he asked, his voice ringing out over the crowded hall.

Rook's heart raced. Oh no. He could see where this

was going. The wolf-guard was distracted by the scene; he jerked his arm out of her grip and stumbled away. He had to get out of here.

"The puck!" Arenthiel intoned, and pointed at him from the platform. "The puck stole the Summerlands crown, delivered it to his puck allies, and has returned to enjoy the chaos he created."

Rook suddenly found himself at the center of a circle of staring Lords and Ladies. Fer stood at the edge, her face pale, eyes wide.

"I didn't—" he started to protest. He looked desperately for an opening, but he was surrounded. Nathe-guards were muscling through the crowd, closing in.

"He was *seen!*" shouted the lead nathe-warden from behind him. "Last night, my fellow wardens and I tracked this puck to the wall, where he met with three other pucks. We pursued him as he returned, but he managed to evade us."

"He must have stolen the crown then," Lord Artos, the bear-man, growled from the platform, "and brought back this false crown to put in its place."

"Look there," the nathe-warden added. She'd come to stand behind him, where she pointed at the long scrape on Rook's leg. "That was left by my arrow as he fled. There can be no doubt of his guilt."

"No!" Rook started to shout, and the nathe-warden

stepped closer and looped her willow-strong arm around his neck, choking off the rest of his protest. He whipped his elbow back, catching her in the face, and as she staggered away he dove for an opening in the surrounding crowd. Two other wardens jumped on him and dragged him back, seizing his arms. He struggled, and they gripped harder, lifting his feet off the ground.

"The puck must be punished for this crime," the bearman said from the platform. He pointed to the door. "Now, take him away!"

✸ ✸ ✸

Fer felt frozen inside, even colder than the glamorie that covered her. Rook had really done it. She'd never really, truly, in her heart believed that he would, but he had. Betrayal. She should be crying now, shouldn't she? But her tears felt frozen; the glamorie wouldn't let them melt and fall.

She stood stunned at the center of a circle of Lords and Ladies. They whispered and stared.

And then the accusations started.

"That half-human girl brought the puck here," Fer heard.

And "She was working with the puck to steal the crown."

And then, "Arenthiel was right—she is a puck, herself."

Up on the platform, the High Ones were whispering

together. Then one of them held up a hand, and Fer felt a wave of power wash over the room. Instantly all the whispers stopped.

Lord Artos, the bear-man, stepped forward. His close-set eyes scanned the room. Seeing Fer, they narrowed. "The High Ones have spoken." His rumbling voice filled the room. "To prove their fitness, the contestants must wear their glamories until morning. The puck will be dealt with then, and the contest will go on. The contestant who recovers the crown will be named the new Lord or Lady of the Summerlands. That is all."

As the Lords and Ladies left the nathewyr, Fer stood alone, like a rock on a beach with the waves drawing away from her.

Gnar and Lich lingered. "Well, Strange One," Gnar asked. "Is this another strange thing you've done?"

"You were working with the puck?" Lich asked in a low voice.

"No," Fer whispered. "I wasn't. I trusted him, and he betrayed me."

"Of *course* the puck betrayed you," Gnar said, as if Fer was the stupidest person she'd ever met. "It is their nature to betray all but their own kind. It is what they are, as we are what we are, and humans are what you are. You put a burden on him expecting differently. You should have known."

"A *true* Lady would have known," Lich added. He and Gnar left, Lich casting one last look at her over his shoulder.

Maybe she should have known. She had been too trusting. Too slow to figure out how things really worked here. Too . . . human.

And then she was alone in the echoing hall. She looked up at the silvery branches holding up the ceiling. She couldn't possibly win the contest now, no matter what the High Ones had said to her about winning and losing. If the contest really was a test, as they'd written, then she'd failed it. If the High Ones really believed she'd been working with Rook, they'd cast her back into the human world and close the Ways to her forever. What was she going to *do*?

"They will kill him for this," came a smooth voice from behind her.

She turned. Arenthiel had closed the double doors leading into the nathewyr and stood leaning against them.

"The puck deserves death for what he has done, don't you think?" he went on.

Fer shook her head. Rook was a puck, and she was pretty sure she understood now what that meant, but he didn't deserve to die for it.

Arenthiel straightened and paced toward her. "I can save him for you."

She stared at him. When she spoke, her lips felt stiff. "What?"

"I will ensure that the High Ones do not pronounce a sentence of death upon the puck."

She frowned. Arenthiel was not her friend; he couldn't really want to help her, or Rook. "How will you manage that?"

"I am not a Lord, but the High Ones and I are kin, of a sort." He gave a graceful shrug. "I can speak for your puck, and they will listen."

Fer took a deep breath, letting the glamorie spark a chill over her skin, welcoming the way it helped her think more calmly, more clearly. "Why would you help me?"

"Ah." Arenthiel pointed at Fer's head. "That crown you are wearing."

Fer reached up with cold fingers; she felt leaves, twigs, the leafy crown still on her head.

"It is a true crown," he explained. "You are meant to be the Lady of the Summerlands. You would already be the Lady if you had accepted your people's oaths. The High Ones, I suspect, know this, but they do not know what to do about the lack of oaths between you and your people, or about your human side, and so they called us all here, not to run a true contest, but to test you. To be sure that you really are worthy."

The contest is a test, they'd written. In her bones, Fer felt the rightness of what he said. She *was* the true Lady. "But I'm failing," she said. "I lost both parts of the contest."

"Do you think so?" Aren gave a graceful shrug. "Maybe, maybe not. It is difficult to know what the High Ones are planning. You think in lines, and they think in circles; you are a fool, and they are wise. Yet we are kin, of a sort, and sometimes I can perceive their meaning. It has occurred to me that perhaps you are winning, after all. I am willing to take the chance that you are. For it would not be a bad thing at all, to have the true Lady of the Summerlands owe me a favor."

Again what he said made a cold kind of sense. "All right," she said slowly. "A favor for a favor. I could do that."

Arenthiel raised a slim finger, as if chiding her. "But Gwynnefar, you know the rules that govern our lands. I know that you do not like oaths. Still, you must swear." And then he smiled his beautiful smile, but now it had an edge on it like the sharpest of knives. With his clear puck-vision, Fer realized, Rook had seen the knife in that smile all along. "You must swear an oath," Arenthiel went on, "to owe me this favor. This one little service. Will you swear?"

Swear him an oath? Oh, he'd backed her into a corner, hadn't he? But it was to save Rook's life. She really didn't have any choice. Did she? Her thoughts whirled, and then, thanks to the chill of the glamorie, calmed. She shook her head. "I, um . . ." she said slowly, ". . . I need some time to think about it."

For a second it seemed as if Arenthiel was furiously angry, like the moment before lightning flashes out from a thundercloud. Then the moment passed. "Well, then!" he said brightly. "You will tell me in the morning, when the punishment of the puck is to be decided. If you will swear to owe me this one service, you will not have to see the puck die."

* * *

The nathe-wardens dragged Rook through the nathe's passages and then hustled him down a narrow, winding staircase that burrowed like a root deeper and deeper underground. Only a few dull crystals lit the stair; the wardens hulked up like shadows before him and after him, their grips like iron on his arms. Fer's bee came too, tickling where it clung to his neck, but he couldn't get a hand loose to brush it off. The walls were wood, and then, as they went deeper, they were packed dirt, and the air grew damp and heavy.

At last the staircase ended in a hole full of shadows.

They weren't going to put him in *there*, were they? Horrified, he yelled and hit out, and the wardens grabbed him and shoved him, still struggling, off the end of the stairs.

It wasn't a long drop, just a little over his own height. He hit the bottom and leaped up, scrabbling with his fingers at the edge of the hole so he could climb out, but the warden kicked them off and then bent and did something with her hand against the ground, and thick vines grew, erupting from the dirt and stretching across the opening like bars.

He jumped up again and gripped the vine-bars, shaking at them, but they were solid. He dropped back to the bottom of the cell, the hard-packed dirt cold under his bare feet. Above him, the wardens stared down, dark shadows framed by the dim light of the crystal in a niche in the wall behind them. One of them said something in a low voice, and the other warden nodded.

"Let me out of here!" he shouted. "I didn't do it!"

Ignoring him, they turned and started up the narrow stairs.

"No!" he shouted, despairing, but they were gone. They were never coming back, were they? And there was *no way out*. He was stuck here. Stuck! There wasn't much room for pacing; the cell was just two steps wide.

He thought of the shifter-bone in his pocket, but there wasn't enough space for his horse-form, so he couldn't kick his way out.

Maybe he could dig a hole. With his fingernails he scraped at the dirt around the vine-bars, but it was almost as hard as rock.

A long time later, his fingernails were cracked and his fingers black with dirt, and he'd scraped away a dent about as long as his thumb. Then he froze, hearing footsteps on the stairs.

Two feet wearing soft deerskin boots came down the steps, and then Arenthiel crouched at the edge of Rook's cell, looking down at him.

Rook felt a growl building in his chest. Without warning, he leaped up and grabbed through the bars for a grip on the other boy. Arenthiel flung himself back, out of reach, scrambling away, stumbling against the stairs.

Rook fell back into the cell, panting, and got ready to spring again.

Arenthiel got to his feet, examining the palms of his hands, then brushing them off on his long embroidered silk coat. "My goodness," he said calmly. "I suppose I should have expected that." He crouched on the steps again, farther away this time, and gave Rook a bright smile. "I want to talk to you, Robin. Are you going to listen to me?"

Rook didn't answer. With one hand he gripped one of the vine-bars, then hoisted himself up to make a grab with his other hand at the other boy's ankle. Out of reach, curse it. He fell back again, growling.

"Well, then," Arenthiel said, with a mock-sad sigh. "I suppose I'll have to find some way to keep you still." He leaned forward and placed a hand flat on the last stair. He closed his eyes and muttered something under his breath.

Rook felt something nudge his foot. He jerked around and saw a gray, scaly-skinned root as thick as a wolf-guard's muscled arm breaking through the hard-packed floor, questing toward him like a blind snake. He stumbled back, and another root broke from the wall behind him, looping over his shoulder. A third root snaked around his wrist and pinned him to the wall. "Let me go!" he gasped. But the more he struggled, the tighter the roots gripped him.

"Now are you ready to listen?" Arenthiel asked.

"No!" Rook snarled.

Another root twined out of the wall and around Rook's neck, and all of a sudden struggling didn't seem quite as important as just breathing.

"It's all right, Robin, you don't have to answer." Arenthiel settled himself more comfortably on the bottom step. "I've always hated you pucks," he said, wrinkling his nose as if he smelled something nasty. "So messy. So much trouble. And you *see* too much."

It was true—even from down here, Rook could see what Arenthiel really was. Not a boy, but something old and, he was starting to realize, poisonous, somehow. If he squinted, in the dim light Rook could see some kind of darkness in him, almost as if he was rotting at the core. This ancient creature was plotting something, and nobody could see it except for him.

"I've managed to keep it hidden for a long time, but you've seen what I truly am, haven't you?" Arenthiel said. "Do you have any idea how old I am?" He glanced down into the cell. "I suppose a puppy like you couldn't possibly understand. Very old. I have waited a very long time to become Lord of a land, and for the power that would bring me. Then that Mór usurper tried to take over the Summerlands, and I thought, ah!" He held up both hands in mock excitement. "A Lordless land, all mine! I knew I could defeat the Mór and convince the High Ones to give me the Summerlands as a reward. But then"—he shook his head with false sadness—"then your Gwynnefar came, and the Summerlands, which should by rights be mine, went to her instead."

Rook swallowed against the vine holding his neck. "You did it. You stole the crown."

Arenthiel raised his eyebrows. "Of course I did! And made it seem your doing. Well done, wouldn't you say?

And now your Gwynnefar has sworn me an oath. She has bound herself to me."

No. Not Fer. He was lying.

"She did it to save your life, dear Robin."

To save him? Knowing Fer, that could be true. How could she have been so stupid, trusting a creature like Arenthiel? Swearing an oath to him? Stupid, stupid, stupid. Rook strained against the roots that bound him to the wall.

"Oh, don't even bother, Robin," the ancient creature said. "Now, a puck with keen vision like yours could be useful to me, at such a time. If you will bind yourself to me, as your friend did, I will see that you're not put to death."

Swear an oath? Bind himself to Arenthiel? He'd already done that—bound himself to the Mór—and he'd never do it again.

"Well?" Arenthiel asked. His golden eyes glittered in the dim light.

"No," Rook choked out. Death first.

"Oh, alas." Arenthiel got to his feet and straightened his fine coat. "I suppose there's no changing your mind. Not to worry. I don't really need you; it simply would have been convenient. It's too bad about your brother-pucks, though."

His brothers? What did they have to do with any

of this? Rook wanted to shout questions, but the vines around his neck tightened, and then Arenthiel was gone.

The bee that had been watching him for Fer buzzed in a bright circle around the cell and then landed on one of the vines that bound his wrist to the dirt wall.

He eyed it. "Here, you bee."

It flicked its wings and gave a low hum.

"Go and find your Lady. Tell her to come get me out of here."

The bee flew off the vine and brushed softly against his face; then it zipped out of the cell and, like a fading spark in the darkness, disappeared up the stairs.

He waited. When Fer came, he could tell her the truth, and surely she'd believe him. She had trusted him once—she *had* to believe him. At least one more time.

But she didn't come.

sixteen

Fer spent the night huddled in the corner of Phouka's stall, shivering at the glamorie's icy touch, seeing again the moment of Rook's betrayal. As the long night ended, she went, taking one of her bees with her, with the Lords and Ladies and Gnar and Lich along the forest path to the vine-wall, where Rook's punishment would be decided. She felt heavy with weariness, and she felt as if a block of ice had frozen inside her. She'd been wearing the glamorie for too long; she needed to take it off. But she couldn't, or she really would lose the competition.

The sky was silver with dawn, and the wide Lake of All Ways glimmered like a huge mirror. Fer stood apart from the other Lords and Ladies, and from Gnar and Lich. The dew soaked into her mother's soft boots, but she felt too numb even to shiver at the early-morning chill in the air. Her bee, the one that had been watching Rook for her, had come back; it had buzzed and bumbled at her ear, trying to tell her something, but she still couldn't understand what it was saying. Now it clung to the collar of her shirt next to the other bee. She reached up with a heavy hand to stroke its fuzzy back, and it gave her a reassuring buzz in reply.

The sky grew brighter. Then the gathered people murmured and turned toward the wall, and the vines drew apart and the High Ones glided out. They wore hooded cloaks the same silver color as the sky, and as they walked their feet left no prints on the dewy grass. Behind them came Lord Artos, and then Arenthiel, surveying the scene with glittering eyes; he came to stand beside Fer, almost as if he was guarding her. The High Ones stood, framed by the Lake of All Ways behind them. Their hoods shadowed their faces.

Then the lead nathe-warden stepped through the opening in the vine-wall, followed by two wardens with Rook between them. One more warden came last, carrying four spears tipped with leaf-shaped silver blades. Rook's hands were bound with vines, but he struggled, snarling and snapping at the guards as they dragged him across the grass. The wardens forced him to his knees before the High Ones and Lord Artos, keeping him there with a hand on each of his shoulders. He looked desperately around; seeing Fer standing beside Arenthiel, he fixed his flame-bright eyes on her and didn't look away.

Fer watched him with dull eyes. He was shaking, she could see, frightened despite his fierceness.

A part of her brain was clenched with fright too, and shivering with worry, but the glamorie made her feel far, far away from it.

The whispering Lords and Ladies fell silent. One of the High Ones tipped a hooded head down, nodding at Lord Artos, who stepped forward to speak.

"My Lords and my Ladies," he said, looking around at the crowd. "We bring before us the puck who stole the Summerlands crown and delivered it to his brother-pucks. The proper punishment for such a crime is death."

Fer saw many in the crowd nod at that. They wanted to see Rook die, she realized. Then Arenthiel caught her eye. "If you swear me the oath," he whispered, "you will not have to see the puck put to death." She knew swearing such an oath was wrong, but she couldn't bear to see Rook die. She gave a slow nod, her answer.

Arenthiel left her side, gracefully bowing to the High Ones and then speaking quietly to Lord Artos. Behind her, Fer heard the Lords and Ladies murmuring, wondering why the execution of the puck was being delayed.

Lord Artos nodded, spoke with the High Ones for

a few moments, then addressed the crowd again, with Arenthiel at his side. "The puck will not be killed at this time." Fer heard a sigh of disappointment from the Lords and Ladies as the bear-man went on speaking. "For Arenthiel has made a request on behalf of Gwynnefar that we not kill the puck here today, which the High Ones, in their wisdom, have granted."

Rook was still staring at her, and he didn't look grateful.

"And now, on behalf of the High Ones, I pronounce the puck's sentence." Lord Artos turned and pointed at the Lake of All Ways. "The Way to the human world opens here. The puck will be put through this Way, never to return to these lands."

Fer looked up and met Rook's eyes. His teeth were clenched, she saw, and his face was set.

"Furthermore," Lord Artos went on, "the pucks themselves will be punished for the trickery they dared to bring into the nathe. This afternoon, those who still wish to be named Lord or Lady of the Summerland will compete in the last part of the contest. They will hunt down the pucks. The one who recovers the crown from them shall be the new Lord or Lady. And then every last puck in these lands will be killed."

Fer saw Rook flinch at that, and his face went pale with horror. "No!" he shouted. "They don't have the crown!" He lunged desperately toward her. "Fer, my brothers didn't—" and the warden's fist came down on the side of his head, sending him sprawling onto the wet grass.

"Bring him," the warden ordered, and the two other wardens hauled Rook up and dragged him to the pebbled shore of the lake. They stood him on his feet, holding him upright as he wobbled from the blow. One of the wardens put his hands on the vines, and they dropped from Rook's wrists and lay writhing on the ground. Each of the four wardens had a spear now, and they lowered them, forcing Rook toward the lake.

Arenthiel leaned in and said something to Rook that made the puck snarl back at him. Then Lord Artos knelt and put his pawlike hand on the rippled surface of the water.

He was opening the Way to the human world, Fer realized. Only a Lord or a Lady could do it. The bearman crouched there for long minutes, his shoulders hunched, his bearded face growing tense and lined, the tendons in his hands standing out as if he was pushing hard against something. Sweat beaded on his forehead and dripped from the end of his nose. At last, the ripples on the surface of the lake ironed out. "The Way is open," Lord Artos said in a strained voice.

"Go in, Puck," a warden said sharply.

Rook turned, blinking, and found Fer in the crowd. "I didn't betray you, Fer," he said in a steady voice. "I was going to, but I didn't."

He turned back to the lake.

Fer caught her breath; even the glamorie wasn't enough to stop the horror that was building in her chest. This was wrong. *Wrong.* She remembered the bees clinging to her collar, and she took one of them into her heavy hand. "Go with him," she whispered. The bee bumbled at her fingers, then zoomed through the crowd to Rook.

The wardens closed in with their spears, driving him toward the water. Fer saw Rook flinch away. Without a backward look, he jumped from the pebbled shore into the Way.

And he was gone.

Fer stumbled back to the nathe-palace with the rest of the Lords and Ladies. They cast her suspicious looks and muttered loud enough for her to hear. "She let him in," they hissed. "Human." And ". . . in league with the puck." Arenthiel appeared next to her and said something about swearing an oath to him, but she bowed her head and plodded on.

"Very well," he said sharply, not so friendly anymore. "I will come to you shortly. Prepare yourself."

Finally she made it to her rooms.

"Are you all right, Lady?" Fray asked, meeting her at the door.

Fer just stared at her.

"Come in," Twig said, gently taking her hands and leading her into the room.

She found herself sitting on the cushion by the low table. The bee buzzed from her collar and circled her head, round and round. Fray and Twig were talking, their voices a muddle to her tired ears. She looked down at her hands in her lap, and they looked pale, the fingernails tinged with blue.

The glamorie. Contest or not, she had to get it off. She closed her eyes and summoned every scrap of her own will. Passing her cold fingers over her arm, she felt for the net of glamorie. She felt its chill sparkle but no edge.

Gritting her teeth, Fer pushed her fingertips against the net of the glamorie. She gasped as the net tore; its edges slithered away from her fingers. Fer seized an edge and pulled, and slowly, slowly, a sliver of the glamorie peeled off her arm. Its icy fishhooks had set themselves into her; they'd grown through her skin and deep into her bones.

Bit by painful bit she peeled off the rest of the glamorie until it lay like a pile of broken glass on the low table before her. Her heart pounded as if she'd been running through the woods with the Mór and all of her hunters in pursuit. Exhausted, she put her head down on her arms. All the frozen tears inside her melted at once, and she cried until the sleeves of her mother's coat were wet.

Once all the tears were gone, she lifted her head, sniffling, wiping the tears off her face. It was funny how crying actually made her feel better.

Twig and Fray were watching her, their eyes wide. The bee hovered before her, almost as if it was worried.

"I'm okay," she croaked. She looked at the glamorie, shimmering like moonlight on the tabletop. "Twig, get the box."

The fox-girl nodded and darted into Fer's room, coming back with the little wooden box.

With the tips of her fingers, Fer picked up the glamorie and dropped it into the box. She closed the lid and gave a great, shuddering sigh. Every Lord and Lady of the nathe wore a glamorie, and it made them cold and heartless.

"I will never be that kind of Lady," she whispered to herself. Even if it meant losing the contest and going back to the human world, she would never wear the glamorie again.

Arenthiel would come soon to demand her oath. To get ready, Fer put on her jeans, T-shirt, and patch-jacket. They were her simpler clothes, but they were her strength, too—her armor. The stick-people brought food, but she couldn't eat. Fray and Twig watched as she paced nervously across the room. The bee buzzed back and forth, just as agitated.

"What did they do with the puck?" Fray asked.

The thought of Rook's punishment made her stomach clench. But maybe it wouldn't be too awful. The Way that led to the human world came out not too far from Grand-Jane's house; she might help him. "Arenthiel promised me he would speak to the High Ones. Instead of killing Rook, he got them to put him through the Way into the human world."

At that, Fray and Twig exchanged a glance. "That Arenthiel promised to save the puck?" Fray asked sharply.

Fer nodded. Maybe Fray didn't like that idea. "Do you think Rook really stole the crown?" The question had been nagging at her.

Fray shrugged. "He slipped away that night. He could have done it then."

Yes, he could. The glamorie had made her thoughts as clear as icicles, and as cold, and then it'd seemed like he'd done it, but now she wasn't so sure. *I didn't betray you, Fer*, he'd said on the edge of the Way. What if he really hadn't?

"Lady," Fray said, looking grim. "What words did

Arenthiel say when he promised to help you save the puck?"

What words? "He promised . . ." Fer paused, trying to remember exactly what Arenthiel had said, when there was a heavy knocking and the door burst open.

Arenthiel strode into the room followed by a willowy nathe-warden. The warden slammed the door and stood in front of it, blocking the way out.

Rook wouldn't like this, Fer found herself thinking. It was too much like a trap.

"Gwynnefar!" Arenthiel exclaimed, smiling widely and holding out his hands to Fer.

She stood staring at him. She wasn't going to play his game, pretending to be his friend. Slowly Fer crossed the room to Aren and stood before him, her heart pounding. Didn't his cheeks get sore, she wondered, smiling so much?

He looked her over, eyebrows raised. "Oh, you are not wearing the glamorie. It really is too bad, Gwynnefar. With the glamorie you are"—he waved his hand airily—"quite lovely. Worthy to rule. To take it off is to admit failure. And without it, I am sorry to say, you look rather dowdily human." His mouth turned down into an exaggerated pout.

"I don't care what you think," Fer said firmly. "I

won't wear the glamorie again."

For just a moment, she thought she saw a hard gleam in his eye, but then he was beaming again. "Well, you know why I am here!"

She nodded slowly, her stomach sinking. "You saved Rook, so I owe you an oath of service."

"Yes." He gave a graceful nod. "Gwynnefar, I must tell you how much danger you are in. I have been visited by several Lords and Ladies of the nathe." He lowered his voice, speaking confidingly. "They are certain that you were in league with the puck all along. Why else would you have brought him here, they ask! It is only a matter of time before they convince the High Ones to imprison you. But once you have sworn an oath of service to me—the oath you owe me, my dear—I will be able to protect you, just as I protected your puck."

She swallowed down a lump of fright. If she swore this oath, it meant she'd have to do whatever Arenthiel ordered her to, which made her feel cold and shivery inside. What if he ordered her to put on the glamorie again?

But she'd promised. . . .

Aren saw her hesitation. "My dear, you don't want to oppose me," he said, still smiling that knife-edged smile.

Fer shook her head. The bee bumped up against her ear, buzzing sharply. *Zmmmmmrmnm*, it said, as if it was trying to tell her something. She brushed it away. "You saved Rook, just like you promised, so I will swear the oath."

"Ah!" Arenthiel clapped his hands. "Lovely. You are a Lady, a true and noble Lady, and I know you will serve me well."

Taking a deep breath, Fer started. "I, Gwynnefar of the—"

"On your knees, I think," Arenthiel interrupted.

Oh. She knelt on the hard floor and gazed up at him. When she spoke, the words tasted like ashes in her mouth. "I, Gwynnefar—" she started again.

Suddenly Fray loomed up behind Arenthiel. Snarling, the wolf-guard raised her huge fist and brought it crashing down on the top of his head. Arenthiel's golden eyes rolled up, and as he toppled, Fray whirled and leaped at the nathe-warden. The two guards struggled; Fray's big hands wrapped around the warden's throat. Twig was blocking the door, tiny and fierce.

Fer scrambled to her feet. What were they *doing*?

Fray drew back her fist and smashed it into the warden's face; the warden crumpled to the floor, greenish blood spraying from her nose. The wolf-guard stood over her, fist raised, but the warden stayed down with her eyes closed.

"Fray!" Fer gasped.

Fray turned. "He was lying, Lady," she snarled, pointing at Arenthiel, who lay unconscious at Fer's feet.

"Lying!" Twig added from the door.

All Fer could do was stare at them. The bee buzzed back to her collar and settled there, vibrating with alarm.

"What did he say about saving the puck?" Fray asked grimly.

The same thing Fray had wanted to know before. Fer's thoughts scrambled for an answer. "He said, um . . ." It had been in the nathewyr, and Arenthiel had said . . . "He said if I swore him an oath, he wouldn't let the High Ones . . ." She slowed as she realized what Aren had actually promised. "He wouldn't let the High Ones pronounce a sentence of death. And they didn't. The High Ones didn't pronounce anything at all, *Lord Artos* did. And then he said that I would not have to watch Rook die." She gazed in horror at Fray. "What does that mean?"

"They put the puck through a Way to your world, Lady," Fray answered. "He can't live there for very long. Arenthiel sent the puck into the human world to die."

seventeen

Fer's heart jolted. Rook *dead*?

She couldn't even imagine such a thing. Rook was too annoyingly, growlingly, stubbornly alive to be dead.

"How long?" she asked, her voice shaking. "How long until he dies?"

Fray shrugged. "Dunno, Lady. Not very long. My mother told me stories about it, said our kind, we can live in the human land for a little while, but then what I hear is anyone stuck over there for too long fades away until he's gone."

Fer took a deep, steadying breath. She was done crying. Now it was time to do something, before it was too late. She stepped over Arenthiel's unconscious form and met Fray and Twig in the middle of the room. "Fray, we have to go."

"Lady, he still could have done it," the wolf-guard said.

Rook could have stolen the crown, she meant. "No," Fer shook her head. She felt a sudden fierce loyalty to Rook. He'd been trying to tell her, all along, what it meant to be a puck, and now she thought she knew. He and all the other pucks—they were outcast, but it wasn't because they were bad. It was because they would never let anyone *rule* them.

Maybe Arenthiel had been right. Maybe Fer *was* dangerous; maybe she was a bit of a puck herself. She knew Rook must have come to the nathe with her to steal the crown, but when he said he hadn't betrayed her, she believed him.

"I think Arenthiel did it," Fer said, pointing to him. "He cheated before, starting the contest early. I think he's cheating again, stealing the crown to win." She thought back. "He must have been planning from the start to make it look like Rook was the thief." That explained why he'd been so interested in Rook when they'd first met. A puck was the perfect person to accuse—everyone would believe the worst of him.

She'd believed the worst too. It made her heart hurt. *And* it made her determined to save him.

"Fray, we have to go now," she ordered. "Go to the stables and get Phouka ready, and Twig's mount and the bees. Twig and I will get our stuff together here. We'll meet you at the path that leads to the vine-wall."

"Where are we going to, Lady?" Fray asked. "Will you go to the human world to bring back the puck?"

That's what she wanted to do. But she had something else she had to do first, the thing Rook would want her to do, if he were here.

"He's going to wake up," she said, poking at Arenthiel with her toe, "and he's going to go after the pucks. He wants to hunt them and kill them, every last one. He must have suggested it to Lord Artos when they sent Rook away." The bee hummed approvingly at her ear. "I do have to save Rook, but first we have to go to his brother-pucks and warn them that the hunt is coming."

"But Lady, we don't know where the pucks are," Fray protested.

"Don't worry," Fer said, heading to the bedroom with Twig. "I know how to find them. Now hurry! Go!"

Leaving Arenthiel and the warden, who were lying on the floor, groaning themselves awake, Fer raced down the stairs carrying her stuffed saddlebags; Twig followed with two bags of her own. It was the middle of the morning and the hallways of the nathe were crowded.

Better to go slowly, to not attract attention. Fer edged past clots of Lords and Ladies and ducked by wardens until she reached the outer doors.

It was raining, a light drizzle that made the gnarled stairs slippery. Fer was glad for her sneakers as she leaped down the steps and then splashed across the puddled courtyard.

"Come on!" she shouted to Twig, who was panting behind her. Together they ran across the sopping-wet grass, leaving the rain-damp nathe looming behind them, until they reached the path that led into the forest.

Fray was there with Twig's curly-horned white goat, a stamping, nervous-looking Phouka, and a swarm of very excited bees.

"Hurry," she urged, tossing the saddlebags to Fray and swinging herself onto Phouka's back. He danced sideways, and she patted his neck to calm him. Fray climbed awkwardly on behind her, and Fer glanced over to see Twig clinging to her mount's back. "To the wall, Phouka," she said.

They dashed through the forest, the bees streaming behind them. The dripping trees leaned over them and crowded the path, and Fer urged Phouka to run—*faster, faster*. Arenthiel might be awake by now, and if he was he'd gather the hunt and come after them quickly. At last they reached the vine-wall, where Fer slid from

Phouka's back, hurried to the wall, and put her hand on it. As before, the vines unwove themselves and parted like a curtain. Fer climbed onto Phouka and they went through, the vines knitting closed behind them. "To the Lake of All Ways," Fer ordered. With a whinny, Phouka galloped over the grass to the pebbly shore of the lake.

Catching her breath, Fer called the bees to her. They buzzed loudly, swirling in frantic circles around her, glistening in the misty rain. Phouka twitched and flicked his tail. "You've been sharing a stall with them for days, Phouka," Fer chided. "Just calm down." She climbed off his back and ran closer to the water, her feet crunching on the pebbled shore. Fer turned her attention to the bees, drawing them closer with a wave of her hand. They wove together like a golden net, and their buzzing quieted as she spoke. "I need you to find the pucks," she said. At that, Phouka gave a sharp whinny. He didn't know that Arenthiel was planning to hunt his brother-pucks, or what had happened to Rook. "I know, Phouka," Fer said more loudly. "I'll explain in a minute."

The lake lay before her like a wide, silver mirror clouded by smudges of mist. Tiny wavelets lapped against the shore, making a *rush-rush* sound against the pebbles. She crouched and rested her fingertips against the pearly smooth surface of the water. Stillness spread from her hands, and the waves stopped rippling.

This lake was the meeting of all Ways—all the Ways that led from one part of the lands to another, and the Way that led to the human world. She wanted to go through and fetch Rook, but there wasn't enough time. First she had to find out what land the pucks were hiding in. Closing her eyes, feeling the power in her hands, she opened all the Ways at the same time. "Go," she whispered to the bees. "As fast as you can, find the pucks and come back. I'll open the Ways for you when you return."

Like golden arrows, the bees shot high into the air, turned in a graceful arc, and zoomed down toward the surface of the lake. Each bee plunged through the curtain of the water and disappeared into a different Way.

Fer stood and wiped her fingers on her damp jacket. Rain sifted down from the gray sky. She glanced back at the vine-wall, not far away. Beyond the wall, all seemed quiet. Arenthiel wasn't after them yet, but it wouldn't be long. "Hurry, bees," she whispered, and went to explain to Phouka what had happened to Rook and why she had to get to his brother-pucks as soon as she possibly could.

eighteen

The rain got heavier, until Fer was soaked and water was dripping from the end of her braid. Twig sat hunched on the back of her sodden mount, and Phouka stood with his head down, staring fixedly at the lake, Fray beside him.

Worry about Rook rattled around inside Fer and made her pace along the edge of the lake, kicking at pebbles. What was he doing right now? The kind of trouble he could get into in the human world was very scary and serious. Even in the countryside where Grand-Jane lived, there were dangerous weapons, and cars that ran people over, and people who wouldn't understand what a puck was. And time passed far more quickly in the human world than here. Rook had been gone for only a little while, but that would be at least several days in that world, which meant she had to get to him fast, before he started to fade.

She felt a buzzing in her bones—the bees were back. She bent over the water and opened the Ways, and the bees smashed through the gleaming surface of the lake and swarmed around her. Blinking droplets of rain from her eyelashes, Fer watched as they hovered, waiting to lead her through the right Way. A buzzing from her collar, and she looked down. "Okay," she whispered to the fat bee perched there. "Will you wait here?" she whispered, and held out her finger for the bee to crawl onto. "Come and warn me when Arenthiel and the hunt are coming, all right?"

The bee buzzed and lifted off her finger, then flew back toward the nathe.

"Come on!" she called over her shoulder, and Phouka trotted up to her with Fray already on her back. Fer mounted up before the wolf-guard. The bees gathered in a tight swarm, then zoomed off over the lake. Phouka and Twig's mount leaped to follow, and as they hung for just a moment over the water, Fer opened the Way, and they went through.

Going through this Way was like pushing through a lacy curtain of spiderwebs, all gray and sticky. Fer put her head down and clung to the horse's back, and at last they were through and Phouka's hooves landed in crunchy, brown leaves. No summerland, this. The air was chilly, and the sun was setting behind bare-branched trees. "Follow the bees," Fer said to Phouka, and he trotted on, the bees a bright spark in the dark forest they'd landed in.

The bees led them to a cliff wall.

"Here?" she asked, slipping off Phouka's back.

Zmmmmrmmmmmzm, the bees answered, and somehow Fer knew they were saying *yes.*

Shivering in her wet jacket, Fer crunched through fallen leaves to the wall. The long shadows of sunset showed her a path, dark against the paler gray of the cliff. No, not a path, just the barest ledge. Following it with her eyes, she saw that it led up the cliff to what looked like a darker patch, maybe an opening.

"Wait for me here," she ordered, and edged onto the path.

"Lady—" Fray protested.

"I know," Fer said, glancing at them over her shoulder. Her bees hovered overhead. Fray was standing with her arms folded, looking stern; Twig stood beside her in the same position, with the same expression on her sharp little face. Thanks to the thread that connected them, she could feel their worry about what the pucks would do when she barged into their home.

"Don't worry. I'm just going to warn them. I'll be careful, and I'll be back as soon as I can." She gave them a quick, reassuring smile and turned back to the cliff. She felt their eyes on her as she made her way up the path, keeping herself pressed against the wall, feeling for good footing with her sneakers, clinging to little knobs of stone to keep herself from toppling off. At last she reached the patch of darkness and saw that it was an opening. Carefully she crouched and crawled through a short tunnel, and then she peered into a cave full of pucks and shadows.

The cave had sand-colored walls, and it was lit by a few torches and a dying campfire. Smudges of woodsmoke hung below the cave's high ceiling; the air smelled of the smoke and of wet fur and old sweat.

It was strange how all the pucks really did look like brothers. From where she crouched in the dark entrance, Fer counted about twenty of them. Some were taller or shorter or broader or thinner; some had browner or paler or green-tinged skin; there was one toddler puck and two old-man pucks, but they all had black hair and eyes the color of flame. They were busy packing up their things—stuffing bits of ragged clothing into bags and tying blankets into bundles.

As Fer crawled out of the tunnel and got to her feet, one of the pucks saw her and shouted a warning that echoed around the cave, and then all the pucks leaped to their feet, crowding toward her. One fierce puck, dressed only in swirls of black and red paint, lunged forward, grabbed Fer by the front of her patch-jacket, and slammed her against the wall.

"Wait—" Fer gasped.

"Who are you," snarled the puck. "What are you doing here?"

And then her bees were boiling out of the tunnel behind her, their buzzing loud and angry. Three of them swooped in and stung the painted puck on the arms, and he let her go and stumbled back, snapping and swatting at the bees. The pucks, some shifting into their black dog forms, surged forward again, and her bees swarmed into a glittering, golden net in front of her. One of the dog-pucks edged closer, and a bee darted forward and stung him on the nose. He yelped and scrambled back.

Fer caught her breath and pushed away from the cave wall. The bees were giving her time to escape, but she wouldn't give up that easily. She raised a hand, and the bees quieted, pulling back to hover over her head like a buzzing golden crown. "My name is Fer," she said to the crowd of growling, shifting pucks. "I'm a friend of Rook's and—"

"That's a lie," said a tall puck with beads and bits of shiny glass woven into his long braids. He strode forward and gave her an ironic bow. "You're a Lady. You're no friend of any puck."

"Yes, I am." She spoke louder, so they could all hear. "Rook is in trouble."

"He's a puck," the tall one sneered. "Of course he is."

"Not puck trouble," Fer shot back. "Something else."

The pucks were like a wall. They stood mute and firm. "Go away," said the tall puck.

She didn't have time for this. Rook was in the human world, fading away with every minute that passed, and she had to go find him. What would convince them?

Carefully, watching the pucks to see what they would do, she stepped forward. The pucks faded back, leaving the smallest puck standing at the edge of the crowd, gazing up at her with his thumb in his mouth. Coming a little closer, she crouched and held her hand out to him. "Hi," she said softly.

The little puck took his thumb out of his mouth and growled fiercely.

She couldn't help but smile at that; he was so cute. With a flick of her fingers, she called a bee out of the swarm hovering over her head. The bee floated toward the baby puck and brushed softly against his cheek. The baby puck's eyes went wide. "I just want to help you," Fer said.

At that, the pucks muttered and frowned.

She tried something that Grand-Jane did when she really wanted Fer to listen—she lowered her voice, and she felt the crowd of pucks leaning closer to hear. "Arenthiel stole the silver crown that's supposed to be awarded to the winner of a contest to name the new Lord or Lady of the Summerlands. Then he accused Rook and you pucks of doing it, and as punishment he had Rook sent through to the human world. I have to hurry. Rook will die if I don't go get him soon." More stirring and growling at that.

She looked up at the frowning puck, the one with the braids and an ashy-gray tinge to his skin—he seemed like their leader. "Arenthiel is gathering a hunt."

To her surprise, the pucks didn't react at this. The leader-puck just shrugged.

Fer got to her feet and looked around the cave again. The pucks had been packing up when she'd come in. "Did you already know all this?" she asked.

One of the other pucks stepped forward. He had long, tangled hair like a mane down his back, and he wore a tattered yellow cloth wrapped around his waist. "There's always one of your kind after us. It's sport for you Lords and Ladies to burn out a nest of pucks."

"Don't talk to her, Tatter," growled the leader-puck.

The puck named Tatter gave her a quick, mocking grin.

"I don't think you understand," Fer said. "Arenthiel has convinced the whole nathe that you stole the crown. They're not just going to chase you out, they're going to hunt you until they find this crown—which I know you don't have, but they think you do—and when they've caught you, they're going to kill every one of you." She looked around at them, and now their faces showed alarm and fear.

The leader lowered his head and glared in a way that reminded her sharply of Rook. "What happens to us is none of your business," he growled.

"Yes, it is," she said. "Rook is my best friend. I have to save him, and I have to help you. Don't you see?"

They were all staring at her. She heard a couple of growls. No, they didn't see.

Fer sighed. "You're pucks and you don't understand how Rook could be friends with somebody like me. Fine." She backed toward the cave entrance. "Go and run away and do whatever you're going to do. Just don't let Arenthiel's hunt catch you. I'm going to find Rook." She crouched to go through the tunnel to get outside, and then she froze. Her bees buzzed, loud in her ears, and they were trying to tell her something. *ZZZZZmmmmRmMMmmmzm.*

Wait. The pucks had no place to go, did they?

She turned to face them. They reminded her so much of Rook, the way they stood all tense and wary, and the quick grin Tatter had given her.

"You can come to my land—to the Summerlands," she found herself saying. "I'll take you. You'll be safe there until I get back with Rook."

nineteen

Rook fell through the Way. The wind ripped past him and a flurry of stars whirled by, and something brilliantly gold shot past like an arrow, and then he came out into darkness. His feet landed on a hard surface, and he stumbled and sat down with a bump.

"Ow," Rook muttered, and closed his eyes until his head stopped spinning. He heard a low buzz and opened his eyes to see a clearing filled with moonlight, pale as milk. One of Fer's bees settled on the ragged collar of his shirt. He frowned. "What are *you* doing here?"

The bee buzzed, almost as if it was answering.

Rook looked around. To his left was a pond—the Way he'd just come through. On its smooth, dark surface glimmered the reflection of the half-moon overhead.

He rubbed the sore spot on the side of his head where the stupid nathe-warden had hit him, then climbed to his feet. The air felt strange. He didn't know what it was, but it smelled wrong. It was the cool, crisp night air of late autumn, but it was heavy, as if it was leaving a dusting of grime on his skin. "I don't like this," he growled to himself.

Well, it didn't matter if he liked it or not. He was stuck on this side of the Way, in Fer's human world, and that meant he didn't have long before he'd fade away, dead and gone. How long, he wasn't sure.

That snake Arenthiel, he'd gotten exactly what he wanted—the Lords and Ladies of the nathe ready to hunt down the pucks and kill them. Arenthiel, for all he looked young and beautiful, was old and cold and merciless; he'd really do it.

He thought of his brothers—Asher, Tatter, Rip, the little baby, Scrap, all of them. They could all be dead by now. If he were in his dog shape, the thought of losing his brothers would make him howl, long and lonesome.

And Fer, too.

Your friend Gwynnefar has sworn me an oath, Arenthiel had said to him down in the nathe's prison. *She has bound herself to me.*

His brothers, lost. Fer, lost. And there was nothing he could do about any of it.

Shivering, he eyed the pond, the Way that led back to his world. Then he turned his back on it. The Way was closed to him. He'd never see his puck-brothers again, or Phouka, or . . . or anybody else.

Grrrr. Standing here like this was stupid. With the sleeve of his shirt, he wiped off the tears that had gotten onto his face. He'd been in the human world before, and it hadn't felt very good, but it hadn't killed him at once, either. He wasn't dead yet. He had a little time. Maybe there *was* something he could do, even from here.

In the morning, Rook was curled in his dog shape under a bush, watching plumes of steamy breath float up from his nose. This was the longest he'd ever been in the human world. So far he felt all right, except for having been awake all night long, shivering. The nearby pond was slicked with a skin of ice. This human land was edging into winter.

Getting stiffly to his paws, he spat out the shifter-tooth and felt dizzy, not something that usually happened when he shifted. He closed his eyes until the dizziness passed. Opening them in his person shape, his stomach growled. There were probably rabbits in this forest, or some other delicious little animals, but he didn't feel like hunting.

It was time to go out into the human world to search

for Fer's grandmother. She didn't live too far away from here; she'd be easy to find.

The bee Fer had sent with him buzzed in a disconsolate circle around Rook's head, then settled on his shoulder.

"You don't like this place either?" he asked it. The bee was from his own world; maybe it would fade away and die here too.

Rook looked down at his hands, then spread them and held them up to the weak light. They seemed as solid as they ever had. He wasn't sure what the fading was supposed to look like, but he didn't think it was happening yet.

It was early morning, the sky still pink with the rising sun. Over the quiet sounds of dry leaves rustling and the lap of waves in the pond, he heard the murmuring of a stream. The first time he'd been here, Fer had led them out by following that stream. He followed it again, the leaves and dirt icy cold under his bare feet. Shivering, he pulled out his shifter-tooth again and popped it into his mouth. He'd been warmer wearing fur. He felt the dog-shift coming and then . . .

He found himself sprawled on the cold ground. Panting, he got to his four paws, and then fell over again, dizzy. He spat out the shifter-tooth.

After a while in his person shape, the dizziness passed.

All right. So shifting was harder here. It'd probably get even harder the farther from the Way he got. Still, he had to go on.

Unsteadily, he climbed to his feet and followed the stream until it went bubbling through a huge pipe. He scrambled up the bank to a straight road made of small gray rocks. Which way? Fer's bee lifted off his shoulder and buzzed off to the left, then circled back to land on his collar again. Right. If he followed the road to the left, he remembered, it would lead past farms and fields, and after a while it would take him to Fer's grandmother's house. He set out. The rocks were rough on his bare feet, so he walked through the tall dry grasses that rustled at the edge of the road.

The day grew brighter. Strange clouds crossed the sky; they were thin and absolutely straight, as if somebody had drawn a line with white ink across the blue. Human-world clouds, he figured. Another reminder that he was very, very far away from home. On he trudged. From behind, he heard a rumbling sound. He whirled to look and saw, careening along the road, a cart made of metal, with a window at the front.

Quickly he stepped farther off the road. The cart came hurtling toward him, then roared past in a cloud of dust and sooty smoke. As it passed, the smoke settled over Rook's skin like a poisonous curtain. He bent over, coughing.

In a rattle of little stones, the cart lurched to a stop, then backed up.

Rook crouched at the side of the road, coughing into his folded arms. The cart stopped next to him.

He looked up to see a human man poking his head out the cart's side window, frowning down at him. The man had a broad, wrinkled face and wore a bright red shirt and canvas jacket, and he had a cap on his head with a picture of another cart stitched on it. "You okay, kid?" the man asked.

Rook nodded and kept coughing. The cart smoke had hooks in it; it didn't want to let him breathe it out.

"You need a ride somewheres?" the man asked.

Rook shook his head and gave one last cough. Trying to take small breaths so he wasn't breathing in too much of the smoke, he got to his feet. In the back of the cart, a scruffy brown dog poked its nose out another window. It sniffed at Rook, and then broke into frenzied barking.

"Dozer!" the human man shouted at the dog. "You shut up back there, hear?"

The dog strained toward Rook, and its barking grew even more shrill.

Rook felt the hairs on the back of his neck bristle.

"Grrrr," he growled at the little dog, narrowing his eyes.

The dog gave a yelp and cowered away.

"Good dog," the human man said. He looked Rook up and down. "You aren't dressed for this kind of weather, kid. You sure you don't need a ride?"

"I am sure, yes," Rook snapped, backing away. Humans. Always wanting to *help*.

"Ooookay," the man said. "And you got a bee on your shirt." He made the glass go up over his open window, and then the cart zoomed away.

"I know I've got a bee on my shirt," Rook grumbled. Putting his head down, he went on.

After a long, plodding time, he reached Fer's grandmother's house. It was set at the end of a dirt road edged with oak trees bare of leaves. He padded past empty fields, then circled the house, ending up crouched behind a row of white boxes. Beehives, he realized, when Fer's bee gave a happy buzz and was answered by buzzing from inside them.

From where he was hidden, Rook surveyed the house. It was a white box with windows and a gray roof, and it was set in the middle of a square of wiry brown grass. A neatly plotted garden lay near it too, full of withered stalks. Herbs, he guessed. The house wasn't so bad, but the farm fields surrounding it felt soaked with poisons made to kill insects and certain kinds of plants, and make other kinds of plants grow. The air was tainted too. It made his head ache. It was hard to imagine Fer living in such a tamed and tidy place.

He watched as a light went on at a lower window, and he saw a figure cross a room inside. Fer's grandmother. *Grand-Jane*, her name was.

Hm. This could be tricky. He'd met Grand-Jane before. She'd lived near the Way for a long time, long enough to know about magic and about pucks. She didn't like him. Even though she was human, she probably wouldn't want to help him.

A sharp wind blew, and he shivered. Without his fur, he was going to freeze out here. Taking a deep breath, he pulled the shifter-tooth out of the pocket of his ragged shorts and popped it into his mouth. The shift into his dog form came with a swirl of darkness and dizziness that had him shuddering and panting and clinging with his four paws to the ground. Finally it passed.

For the rest of the day, moving from one shadowed place to another, he watched Fer's grandmother. She seemed busy inside her box of a house. The time ticked on. His stomach growled. His head ached. At last, as the wind was growing even more chilly, the sun was setting, and black shadows were creeping across the grassy lawn behind her house, she stepped outside. His ears pricked. She closed the door behind her and came down the steps, crossing the grass toward the beehives.

For a while she was busy doing something with the hives. Rook made his move, getting shakily to his four paws and slinking out of the shadows. When the old woman turned to go back to the house, he was waiting.

Seeing him, she froze. He knew what she saw, a shaggy black dog with flame-bright eyes and a giant bee perched on one ear. Then her eyes widened—she'd realized who he was.

"You," she said. "The puck."

He watched her warily.

"Where is Jennifer?" Grand-Jane asked sharply. She glanced around the yard; she was looking for Fer. "Tell me!"

He backed away. A growl rumbled in his chest. She was dangerous; he could smell that much.

She stepped closer, fierce. "What have you done with her?" She pointed at him with a long, bony finger.

Snarling, he scrambled away, then fled, counting on the growing shadows to hide him.

Grrrr. He'd have to try again in the morning.

twenty

Pucks!

Fer had thought Rook was difficult, with his surly stubbornness, but these pucks were far worse. Before they would consider coming with her to the Summerlands—where they would be safe, she kept reminding them—they had to argue it out among themselves.

"We need to hurry," Fer told them. Time was passing quickly in the other world. Rook needed help—and he needed it now. And she was sure Arenthiel—and Gnar and Lich, she feared, if they were still wearing the glamories—would be starting the hunt very soon. She could *feel* the time slipping away. Why were they being so slow? "Come *on*," she said.

The black-and-red-painted puck bared his teeth at

her, and a few of the other pucks gave her baleful looks. Then they turned back to their huddle around the dying campfire. The painted puck was arguing in low growls with the puck named Tatter, the one with the quick grin like Rook's. The tall leader-puck leaned forward now and then to add something to the argument.

Fer blew out a sigh. They didn't trust her; that was the problem. She opened her mouth to insist that she wasn't a spy, which was what the painted puck seemed to suspect—when she caught a flash of gold out of the corner of her eye.

She whirled to see what it was.

One of her bees came shooting through the cloud of other bees around her and settled at her ear, buzzing and bumbling. It was the bee she'd left behind at the Lake of All Ways.

Arenthiel was coming, it warned.

The rest of her bees hovered over her head, buzzing loudly. "Yes, go," she said. "Find out how close he is." They flowed down to the passageway and out of the cave.

The puck-leader grabbed her shoulder and pushed his face close to hers. "What is it?" he growled.

"My bee saw Arenthiel," she answered, stepping back. "He knows where we are." She turned to face the rest of the pucks. "The hunt is coming. We have to get out of here right now."

"*You* get out of here, Lady," snarled the painted puck. "*We* will fight them!" Several of the other pucks shifted into dogs and bared their teeth.

Stupid pucks!

"No!" she shouted. "If we hurry, we can beat them to the Way out of here." The bee had come quite a distance to report; there was no way Arenthiel and the hunters had gotten themselves armed and saddled up and ready so quickly. She and the pucks still had time to escape.

She grabbed the leader-puck by the arm. Pucks hated traps, she knew. "If we don't hurry, we'll be trapped here."

He jerked his arm out of her grasp and growled.

"Do you all want to die?" she shouted at him, exasperated.

Die—die—die echoed around the cave.

For a second everything in the cave went quiet. As if they really would rather die than give in and trust her.

Fer waited, holding her breath. Now or never, pucks.

Then the leader-puck shrugged. "As it happens, we don't want to die. We'll come." He gave the other pucks a quick nod, and they raced to grab up their things. A few of them helped the old-man pucks, and

Tatter picked up the baby-puck and stuffed him into a knapsack with just his head sticking out. Some of them hurried out the back of the cave; some came with Fer, edging down the side of the darkly shadowed cliff to the ground, where an anxious Fray and Twig waited, and Phouka, who tossed his head and gave a joyful whinny when he saw the other pucks. They shouted back to him—*Finn! Brother!*

The last of the pucks joined them. They started shifting into their dog or horse forms; a few shifted into big black goats with curling horns. Against the black of night, they were a crowd of shadows with fiery eyes.

Fer heard buzzing, and then her bees were there, swirling around her head in a golden swarm. Arenthiel was through the Way, they told her. He would be there soon.

Fer pushed through the jostling crowd of dogs and horses and found the puck-leader. "What do you know about the other Ways leading from this place?" she called. Most lands had more than one Way leading in and out of them, just as a house had more than one door.

"Tatter brought Rook here from your Summerlands. He knows." He shouted for his brother-puck and a black dog bounded up and shifted into the sharply grinning Tatter.

"There's a Way that leads from here to the Summerlands?" Fer asked him quickly.

"Not directly," Tatter answered. "There's one Way leading to another, and then another. It's a bit of a run." He pointed to show her where.

"Just so we stay ahead of the hunt," Fer said. She pushed through the crowd to Phouka; gripping his mane, she swung onto his back. A couple of the dog-pucks growled at that, but Phouka flared his nostrils and pranced. Fer gave Fray her hand and helped the wolf-guard onto Phouka's back too.

From not far away came the high, thin call of a hunting horn.

Fer's heart gave a frightened jolt. Arenthiel's hunt. They were coming. "Come on!" she shouted, and Phouka leaped into a run. Twig and her goat-mount followed, and then the pucks in a galloping, bounding, racing crowd.

She crouched over Phouka's neck and clung with her hands and legs. Twig's quick-hooved goat bobbed along beside her, Twig clinging tightly to its back. From behind, the horn sounded again, closer. "Bees!" Fer called. They zoomed closer. "Scout ahead for the Way," she gasped, pointing in the direction Tatter had shown her, and the bees flew ahead. A moment later they were back, like shooting stars through the night, and they led her to the first Way.

The Way was in the shadow of a huge boulder. It was wide open; they didn't even need her to go first to open it. "Here!" Fer shouted, and she gripped Phouka's mane as he jumped into the shadow. A whirl of blackness and a cold feel of stone and they were through the Way, onto a wide grassland with gray clouds looming over them. Rain poured down. Brushing wet hair out of her eyes, Fer glanced over her shoulder, past Fray's set, pale face, and saw the pucks pour out of the Way, shadows flowing out of a darker shadow.

"Find the next Way," she told the bees, and they flashed ahead again, darting through the silver raindrops. Phouka pounded on through the rain. The pucks surged forward until they were all around her. The next Way was at the bottom of a hill crowded with brambles. They thrashed through it, the Way prickling like thorns, and out into a pine and birch forest with stars overhead that blazed like lanterns.

The ring of hunting horns echoed through the trees.

On they ran. Phouka's flanks were heaving; beside him the pucks were panting. One of them slowed, and they all slowed—brothers, they wouldn't leave anyone behind.

Again, Fer sent her bees ahead. They zipped around the tall pine tree trunks, sparks in the night, then led her to the last Way, a round clearing edged with birch trees. Phouka took the Way in a mighty bound, and it passed in flashes of black and white and tumbling stars, and they touched down in her own land, into the grassy clearing just turning from day into night.

Phouka staggered, and Fer slid off his back. Her own connection with her land flowed up from the ground; she felt it all, from the blades of grass to the wind in the very tops of the trees, to the wide-open Way with the exhausted pucks stumbling through.

From the other side, the faint call of the hunting horns.

The Way would close again when night had fallen. "Hurry!" she shouted.

Another puck came through, then another, a goat who spat out a bit of shifter-horn and fell to his knees, panting. The leader-puck was last, his long hair tangled, his eyes blazing.

"Is that all of you?" Fer shouted to him.

He lifted his head, scanned the clearing full of pucks. "All," he gasped.

Fer faced the Way. It shimmered before her, pearly pink in the twilight. She raised her arms and spread her fingers wide and laid her hand against the opening. It sparked at her touch. As night fell, she felt the Way close, just like a door locking.

"Good," she said. The Way was shut tight until morning.

It didn't give her much time. But maybe it would be enough.

twenty-one

As night came on, heavy clouds drew in over Fer's grandmother's house, and tiny flakes of snow started to fall. Even in his dog shape, Rook felt the cold creep in under his fur. He lurked around the yard for a while, then found a warmish place under the beehives and settled there.

Inside the house, the rooms went dark, and all was silent. The snow sifted down, fine as ash. He watched it dust the grass and the back steps of the house and the roof. Then a wind came along and blew the dusty flakes into a whirl. He shivered and rested his muzzle on his front paws. Fer's bee nestled inside his ear. It tickled, but at least the bee would be warmer.

He hadn't slept the night before, and he was hungry

enough to eat ten rabbits and tired enough to curl up in a corner and sleep for days, but his body felt like a rope stretched tight and about to break. He closed his eyes, but sleep wouldn't come.

All night he watched. Then all the next day and all the next long, long, sleepless night.

By his third morning in the human world, he felt not like a dog, but a starveling stone statue of a dog, still and frozen.

The sky was lightening to gray when the back door of the house creaked open. Fer's grandmother stepped out, then cast a sharp look around the yard. He kept to the shadows where she couldn't see him.

She breathed out steam in the cold air, and Rook expected her to go back into the house, but instead she pulled a blanket over her shoulders and sat down on the steps.

"I know you're out there, Rook," she said quietly, but loud enough for his dog-ears to hear.

Grrrr. Fer must have told her his true name.

"Come out from where you're hiding," she called.

Rook got stiffly to his paws and eased out from under the beehives. Warily, he edged toward the house, his paws crunching on the snow-dusted grass.

She spotted him at once and got to her feet. "Change yourself," she ordered sharply.

He froze. What?

"I won't talk to you in your dog shape," she said. "I'm going to ask you questions, and I want answers."

Oh. Nothing else for it, then. He spat out the shifter-tooth, and the change hit him like a brick to the head. He came out of the darkness to find his cheek pressed to the icy ground; turning his head, he saw Grand-Jane's boots, standing right next to him. He looked up, and up, and there was her stern face, scowling down at him.

"What's the matter with you?" she asked.

He didn't answer, just pulled himself into a crouch, shivering, his head still spinning. Fer's bee circled him once, then settled onto his sleeve, as if it was tired too.

"Where is Jennifer?" Grand-Jane asked.

He shook his head.

He heard her take a sharp breath. "Is she all right?"

"She's—" He coughed. "She's in trouble."

A silence. Grand-Jane making up her mind, he guessed, about whether to believe him or not. Then, a sigh. "You'd better come inside." She turned, and he watched her booted feet pace across the grass, then up the stairs and into the house. The door stayed open.

He really, really didn't want to go into the house. The bee gave an encouraging buzz. "All right," he muttered. Maybe he'd be better off in there than turning into a frozen statue out here. And maybe she'd give him something to eat. After dragging himself to his feet, he followed Grand-Jane inside.

The room was as he remembered from the last time he'd been here. Bright colors, a rag rug on the floor, a square box humming in the corner, a row of magical herbs along a windowsill. And it was warm.

He closed the door and leaned wearily against the wall next to it.

Fer's grandmother faced him across the room. She said something, but he was too tired to make sense of her words. All he could do was stare at her. With an irritated huff, she pointed at a chair next to a table, then went to the noisy box and took some things out of it.

He stumbled over to the chair and sat down, watching her. She'd taken out eggs and butter, and then pulled out a pan and used some kind of magic to start a fire, and started cooking the eggs.

His nose twitched. The cooking food smelled delicious. She cut a slice of bread. *You can have the slice*, he wanted to say. *I'll eat the rest of the loaf.*

At last the food was ready, and she dropped a full plate on the table before him, then set down a fork and knife. His stomach growled. It wasn't fresh rabbits, but it would do.

He spread some butter on a piece of bread and took a big bite. It tasted like ashes, like the old woman had scooped ashes out of a fire pit, molded them into a loaf, and baked it. He choked it down and picked up the fork. Maybe the eggs were all right. He took a bite. The same thing—ashes. He put down the fork and stared at the food.

"What's the matter with it?" Fer's grandmother asked. She stood at the counter, watching him.

He held up his hand. It looked all right, except that it was shaking a little. He clenched it into a fist. So this was how the fading worked. In this world he couldn't eat, and he couldn't sleep, and the air and ground and water were poisonous to him, and that meant it wouldn't be long at all before he was gone.

"Well?" Grand-Jane asked.

Part of him wanted to snarl at her. Stupid human in her tame, deadly, human world. He felt a growl building in his chest.

"Don't you growl at me, Puck," she said, glaring. "I ask you for the third time—where is Jennifer?"

The question asked three times wrenched the answer out of him. "I told you," Rook flared. "She's in trouble." That wasn't enough of an answer, so he went on. "I don't know where she is. In the nathe, maybe. She swore an oath to—" He shook his head. "To something old and evil that wants her land for himself." Suddenly every-thing—the human house, the headache, his hunger and exhaustion—it all came down on him at the same time. Fer was lost. She was on the other side of the Way and the Way was closed, and there was nothing he or her grandmother could do about it.

When Grand-Jane realized he couldn't eat or sleep, she said she'd make up a special tea for him, one that might help.

"It's not going to help," he growled at her.

Ignoring him, she went into a workroom next to her kitchen. He followed, Fer's bee clinging to his collar again. As she put a kettle on another magical fire to boil and started mixing herbs, Rook paced, explaining to her what had happened at the nathe, how Arenthiel had stolen the crown and accused Rook of the crime, and how he'd tricked Fer into swearing him an oath, and that Arenthiel would soon become the Lord of the Summerlands, Fer's land. He didn't even bother telling her the worst of it, that his brother-pucks were being hunted down and killed. "It's already too late to do anything about any of it," he concluded.

"Hmm," Grand-Jane said, and pointed with her chin at a high shelf. "Get that bottle for me."

Rook reached up and grabbed a bottle and set it on the workbench beside her.

"So you say Jennifer swore an oath to this creature,"

Grand-Jane said. She added a pinch of dried leaves to a mortar. "Why did she do that?"

He didn't want to tell her this part of it. "She thought it was to save my life."

Grand-Jane's eyebrows shot up. "She must think very highly of you."

"No," he shot back. "She was being stupid."

"Hmm." Grand-Jane reached for another bag of dried herbs. "Maybe a little peppermint to help with the crankiness." She added it to the mortar, then tipped the mixture into a little cloth bag, which she put into a mug; then she poured in hot water. She turned and leaned back against the workbench and pointed her bony finger at Rook. "Did you see her swear the oath to that creature?"

He blinked. "No. He told me she did."

"Then you're the one being stupid. I don't believe for a second that Jennifer swore an oath to someone as evil as you say. That means she must be fighting him for her land."

He stared at her. Was she right? Was Fer fighting Arenthiel?

She turned and picked up the hot tea and handed it to him. "Now, try this."

The tea tasted awful, like ashes mixed with rotting leaves, but he choked it down, and it made him feel a little less tired and hungry.

"Now," Grand-Jane said firmly, pulling more of her bags of herbs from the shelves. "Jennifer will need our help. The Way is closed to us, but if she opens it and comes here, we must be ready."

twenty-two

Fer stood at the Way, listening. Phouka stood beside her with his head lowered. She heard his snorting breath as he recovered from the run, and the muttering and rustling of the pucks. But nothing from the Way. It was closed, sealed until morning against those who hunted them. Arenthiel was a dire enough enemy, but she'd have to face Gnar and her dragon-mount too, and Lich and his terribly accurate arrows, and both of them were wearing glamories. She wasn't sure how to fight them, let alone defeat them.

"Come, Lady," Fray said from behind her. "You must rest so you will be ready for the morning."

In the clearing, night had fallen. Most of the pucks had shifted back into their person shapes and crouched at one end of the clearing, watching her warily.

Her bees, exhausted, settled onto her hair and shoulders like a golden cloak.

"You all right, Lady Gwynnefar?" came Fray's voice at her shoulder.

Fer nodded. Tired, but okay. And she couldn't think yet about fighting the hunt. She had something else to do first. "I have to get to the Way that leads to the human world."

Fray frowned. "Lady, you must rest, or you won't have the strength to stop Arenthiel from taking this land. You can't risk saving that puck."

"He's my friend, Fray."

"You have other friends," Fray said darkly. "And that puck would have stolen the crown if Arenthiel hadn't stolen it first."

"Maybe," Fer answered. "But I can't leave him in the human world to die."

"What about them?" Fray asked, pointing at the pucks, who lurked in a surly crowd on the other side of the clearing.

Oh, they weren't going to like this. "I'll talk to them," Fer said. "Fray, go with Twig to the Lady Tree and start getting everybody ready to fight. I'll be along soon."

After grumbling about leaving Fer alone with the pucks, Fray left with Twig.

Fer headed across the clearing. The resting bees murmured, lifting, then settling again. The leader-puck stepped forward to meet her.

"What's your name?" Fer asked him.

"Robin," he answered shortly.

Of course, Robin. The same name Rook used with people he didn't trust. Must be a puck thing. "And they're all Robin too?" Fer asked waving at the other pucks.

The leader-puck gave her an ironic bow.

Fer refrained from rolling her eyes. Pucks . . . ! "Okay, *Robin*," she said. "The Way is closed, so Arenthiel can't get through until morning with his hunt. That means you have to stay here."

The painted puck stepped up beside them. He spoke to the leader, not to Fer. "We need an escape route."

"The Way is closed," Fer repeated. "There's no way to get into my land, or out."

The painted puck turned to Fer, and a growl rumbled in his chest. "You're trapping us here," he said, his eyes narrowed.

"It's so you'll be safe," Fer shot back. "I'm going into the human world to get Rook, and I'll come back as soon as I can with him, and in the morning this Way will open again and you can leave if you want to." They stared at her. They didn't have to stay to fight Arenthiel with her, she meant. "All right?" she added.

Their only answer was more growling.

Fine. Typical pucks. She spun around and stalked away from them, across the clearing. Phouka was waiting in the shadows on the other side.

"Your brothers are making me crazy," Fer muttered as she swung up onto his back.

He snorted in answer and trotted through the forest, heading for the Lady Tree.

When she got there, she met Fray, waiting with Twig beside her. They both stood with arms folded, looking stubborn. They wanted to come with her, Fray said. Twig nodded.

"You won't be safe in the human world," Fer explained. "You know that. And I need you to stay here and look after the pucks. They're not going to like being trapped here, but it's the only way to keep them safe."

"All right, Lady," Fray agreed. "Do you want us to save that for you?" She pointed at Fer's head.

She put her hand up and felt the twig and leaf crown, still fresh and green under her fingers. "No," she decided. "I'll wear it. And don't worry. I'll be back before morning."

At least, she hoped she would be.

twenty-three

Rook watched as Grand-Jane got to work in her still-room making protective spells, herbs in little bags for him and Fer to wear around their necks. Not for herself, though. She wouldn't go through the Way to his world, she said. Fer had to deal with Arenthiel on her own.

Rook inspected his spell-bag doubtfully.

"It's real magic," Grand-Jane said as she pounded herbs in a mortar.

While she worked, Rook paced from one end of the stillroom to the other. If he stopped moving, the fading would get him. "You can't be sure Fer didn't swear that oath to Arenthiel," he growled.

"She didn't," Grand-Jane growled back at him. "I trust my granddaughter. And so should you."

He thought he did, but he couldn't be absolutely certain Fer was free of the oath, or of the glamorie she'd been wearing when he'd last seen her, or that she would come for him even if she was free. He rubbed his aching head, trying to think clearly. Fer probably still believed that he'd stolen the stupid Summerlands crown. She might have even joined the hunt for his brother-pucks. If she had bound herself to Arenthiel and he ordered it, she wouldn't have any choice but to hunt them.

Thinking about his brothers hurt too much. He growled and paced some more. Fer's bee buzzed fretfully around his head. Then another bee buzzed past his face. He blinked. Two bees? Was he seeing double? A third bee zinged past.

Bees meant Fer. "She's here!"

At the workbench, Grand-Jane dropped a pestle with a crash and stuffed a few last herbs and some other things into a leather pouch. "Quickly!" She hurried to the kitchen door, flung it open, and looked out. "Jennifer!" she called. The afternoon was heavy with gray clouds, and snow was falling too. A cold gust blew in the open door.

There was no answer to her call.

Grand-Jane grabbed his arm. "She must have sent the bees ahead. She'll be coming through the Way. You must get to her as fast as you can." She shoved him out the door and down the steps. "Change into a horse."

"Oh, sure," he grumbled, shivering as his bare feet landed on the snow-dusted grass. "Any more shifts in this place and you'll have to send home my bones in a sack."

"Stop fussing," Grand-Jane ordered. "Are you going to shift or not?"

As an answer his hand went to his pocket; he snatched out his shifter-bone and popped it into his mouth. He stumbled and braced himself against the rush of dizziness as the shift took him, then threw back his head and snorted, knowing she saw standing before her a black horse with a tangled mane and flame-bright eyes. As a horse he could travel swiftly along the straight roads; he'd have to shift again, to his dog form, when he got to the stream that led to the Way.

And after two shifts like that, the fading would get him for sure.

"Take this," Grand-Jane said, knotting a hank of his mane through a strap on the pouch of herbs. "Jennifer will know what to do with it." She raised that terrifying finger of hers again. "And you listen to me, Puck. There will be no betrayals and no trickery. You must trust my granddaughter."

He'd decide that when he saw her.

"Now, run!" Grand-Jane shouted.

And with a snort and a stamp, he was off.

✳ ✳ ✳

Fer had sent her bees ahead to scout. As she fell through the Way, feeling the tumbling blackness that meant she was entering the human world, the bees returned, whirling around her like sparks flying up from a bonfire. On the other side, she fell sprawling on the frozen bank of the pond. Not very Ladylike, she found herself thinking. Of course, she wasn't a Lady in the human world. The oak-leaf crown had slipped over one eye, and she straightened it, then scrambled to her feet, brushing snow off her jeans.

Time moved so fast here—it was winter already. She shook her head, getting her bearings, then realized that she wasn't alone in the clearing. Just stepping off the snowy path that led along the stream was a black dog who had one ear sticking up and one flopped over, flame-bright eyes, and a muzzle full of sharp teeth. He held what looked like a leather pouch in his mouth. Seeing her, he dropped it and stood with his hackles raised, panting as if he'd been running hard.

She felt a huge wave of relief—he wasn't dead yet, anyway. "Rook!" She stepped closer.

The dog lunged toward her, his teeth bared in a snarl.

She backed up, teetering at the edge of the pond. "Rook, it's me!"

The growling deepened.

With a jolt, she remembered. The last time he'd seen her, she'd been wearing the glamorie and her fine Lady clothes, and standing next to Arenthiel as he pronounced a sentence of death on him. No wonder he was suspicious. More suspicious than usual, anyway. "Rook, look at me," she said, holding her arms out. "I'm not wearing the glamorie."

The air around the dog blurred and Rook caught the shifter-tooth in his hand. In his person shape, he staggered back as if dizzy, and crouched on the snowy ground with his head lowered. She stepped closer, and he flinched away, growling fiercely. "Did you swear an oath to Arenthiel?" he asked, his voice rough.

"No, I didn't. He was lying if he told you I did." She shivered, realizing how close she'd come to being bound to him. "I didn't swear the oath. Fray knocked him on the head and she told me that he sent you here to die."

He shook his head, still wary.

What would convince him? Oh. "Rook, your brother-pucks are all right. They're in my land."

He stared at her. "What?"

She nodded. "Your puck-brothers are in the Summerlands," she told him again. And a third time, so he'd know it was true. "Your brothers are alive."

She saw him close his eyes and let out a breath, as if he'd been bracing himself against a terrible weight and it had suddenly been lifted. "You *helped* them, didn't you." He gave a ghost of his sharp grin.

She didn't know why that was funny. "I sent my bees to find them." She went down on her knees in the snow next to Rook. "Once I explained what was going on, they agreed to come with me." It hadn't been quite that easy, but she didn't have time to tell Rook all about it now. She reached out and laid a gentle hand against his shoulder. For once, he didn't flinch away. Probably too tired. "We need to get you back to the Summerlands."

He looked up at her, his eyes shadowed, as if the flame in them was dying. He opened his mouth to say something, but no words came out.

"Come on," she said. She picked up the heavy leather pouch he'd been carrying and stuffed it into her patch-jacket pocket, then grabbed his arm, dragging him up. He wavered to his feet and stood leaning against her; she put her arm around his waist. Half dragging him, she struggled to the edge of the pond. She couldn't put him down to open the Way—hopefully this would work. She reached out her toe and touched the surface of the water.

A dark ripple spread out and Fer stepped into the pond and took them through.

As they tumbled through the Way, leaving the human world, she lost her grip on Rook, and as they entered the Summerlands he went sprawling onto the mossy ground. She went to crouch beside him. Her bees buzzed worriedly around them. Rook lay with his mouth open and his eyes closed, as if he was sleeping. She checked for fever, resting her fingers on his forehead, but his skin was cool. He probably *was* sleeping, after three or four days awake in the human world.

"She's here!" she heard someone shout, and then more shouts. "The Lady! The Lady has come back!"

Fer looked up. It was night; time flowed so slowly here in the Summerlands that only a few moments had passed since she had left. A fire had been lit near the pond, and her people were gathering. All of her people, shadows in the firelight, crowded around the clearing and the pool to see her, murmuring about the fallen puck.

Then Fray and Twig were at her side. Phouka pushed his nose in and snuffled at his puck-brother.

"It's okay, Phouka," she said, patting his neck. "He's just sleeping." She raised her head and called to the pucks who waited in a surly crowd beyond the firelight. "Rook's all right." He was better than all right, really. He looked quite peaceful and content, lying there on his soft bed of moss. She gave her head a wry shake. He was awfully good at getting himself into trouble.

"Lady," Fray interrupted urgently. "Arenthiel and his hunt are trying to break through the other Way, even though it should be closed until morning. You must come at once."

She looked around the clearing, at the Way to the human world, which glimmered with reflected firelight, at her people, who had gathered—Fray and the other wolf-guards, and Twig and her twin sister, Burr, and the deer-women and badger-men, and all the rest of them. The deep-forest kin had come too, the oldest and wisest of the land's people, the ones whose roots grew deepest. And the pucks, lurking in the shadows.

"Let them come," she decided, getting to her feet. "We'll fight them here."

Her people murmured at that, and through the spiderweb threads that connected her to them, she felt their fright but also their determination. They did not want the Summerlands to be ruled by a Lord like Arenthiel. But without their oaths to tie them to her, they were adrift, unsure of their connection to her.

"Lady," Fray pleaded. "You must let us swear our oaths to you, so we can defend you."

Her heart sank. She had resisted taking their oaths for so long. Was it time to give up, and just become the kind of Lady this place, and its rules, demanded? She wouldn't be able to defeat Arenthiel if she didn't.

"Quickly, Lady," Fray urged. "They are coming."

She opened her mouth to say no—and she knew that they would never ask again, that this was the last chance she would have to prove herself the true Lady of this land.

And then she felt it, the answer clicking into place inside her. The other Way was besieged and the hunt would be upon them soon, but she would do this right. Slowly she stepped away from the human-world Way, leaving it behind her, leaving Rook sound asleep beside it. Then, feeling solemn and shaky, she bowed to her people.

She felt their confusion as they all, except for the pucks, bowed back.

"The High Ones called me to the nathe to make me prove myself the true Lady of the Summerlands," she said slowly, thinking it through. "Their kind of Lady takes her people's oaths and rules over them and the land. She wears the glamorie and a silver crown and feels cold inside." Fer nodded, feeling the rightness of what she was about to do. "I won't be that kind of Lady. I will not *rule*. I will never ask for your oaths."

"But Lady Gwynnefar," Fray said, frowning. "We need to swear oaths so we'll be bound to you, so we can fight for you. It is our way and we need to do it *now*."

"We're supposed to serve you," Twig added. "All of the people of the land want this, Lady."

"That's not how it should be," Fer said firmly. "If I am truly your Lady, then I should swear to serve *you*."

As she said the words, the rightness of them swept through her. Yes, that's what she would do. Fer stepped farther into the clearing so her people were all around her. Twig was shorter than she was, and thin as a sapling; Fray towered over them both, even though she wasn't much older than they were. "Give me your hands," Fer said. Wide-eyed, they did. The rest of her people moved closer, crowding into the clearing, around the glimmering Way.

Her bees settled on her head like a crown over the leafy crown she already wore, their wings flickering. She spoke clearly so they could all hear. "I am your Lady and your kin, and I swear to you, Fray, and to you, Twig, and to the deep-forest kin and to all of the people of this land that I will serve you and protect you and help you. If you are injured, I will heal you, and"—she thought quickly—"and when we are attacked I will fight for you. I, Fer, swear this oath." Then, to make it really binding, she added, "I swear it once, twice, three times."

She'd been connected to them all before, a thread as delicate as a spiderweb, but as she spoke the oath the thread became a magical cord of kinship like silvery steel, unbreakable, binding until death. She felt a new awareness of her land, too, from the tiniest bug burrowing into the ground, to the greenest leaf at the top of the tallest tree, from the Ways to the farthest reaches of the forests. She closed her eyes and took a deep breath as the connection washed through her, and she would have staggered, except that she felt as if she was strongly, deeply rooted there, and could never be moved.

Twig's face shone with happiness. "Lady," she whispered.

Fer put her arms around Twig; she felt Fray's strong arms come around them both. Her crown of bees gave a contented buzz. At the edge of the clearing, the deep-forest kin hummed their approval, a sound like wind in high branches.

And overhead, the first gray smudges of dawn appeared in the sky.

It was time. Fer stepped out of Twig's and Fray's embrace and cocked her head, listening to her land. From the other Way, down a path and past the Lady Tree, she felt a shudder. Now that dawn was breaking, Arenthiel and Gnar and Lich and the other Lords and Ladies of the hunt were battering through that other Way. Then came a shuddering in the ground under her feet.

"Be ready!" Fer shouted. "They are coming!"

twenty-four

Arenthiel and his hunt thundered into the clearing, scattering Fer's people. The sun had just leaped into the sky, and in its light the hunt was blindingly tall and golden, and they were armed not just with spears but with their glamories and their power to rule. Arenthiel was at their front, riding his tall golden horse. Blood dripped from slashes on its side—he'd spurred it hard during his hunt. Right behind him rode Gnar on her dragon-mount, carrying a spear, and Lich on his fish-goat, with his long bow drawn. A few other Lords and Ladies were ranked behind them.

Fer's people gathered to face them. Through the bond of her kinship with them, Fer could feel their terror and awe at the glamorie ranged against them. Fray and the other wolf-guards bared their teeth; the rest, weaponless, stood ready to fight. Around the edge of the clearing, tall and treelike and short and stumplike, were the deep-forest kin, standing still and silent.

And, ready to fight alongside her people were the pucks, some in their dog shapes, some as horses, all of them flaming with fierceness. It was right that the pucks were here. They were the ones who knew best how to live without *rule*.

Bows were being drawn; spears were being lowered—the hunt was about to begin.

"Stop!" Fer shouted. Her people made a path for her, and she strode to the front and into the space between her people and Arenthiel and his hunters.

From the lofty heights of his horse, Arenthiel, as beautiful and perfect as ever, looked down at her and gave a careless-sounding laugh. "Well, little *human*," he said. "You had your chance to ally with me, and you failed to take it." His voice sharpened. "Instead, you joined those thieving pucks. So now it falls to us to deal with them as we see fit, and then we will deal with you, and your land will be mine. You have no power to stop us." He pointed at the Way, which shone like a golden mirror in the blazing sunrise. "There is your Way, Gwynnefar. Flee to the human world, where you belong."

Staring up at him, Fer felt something strange welling

up in her. It was anger—fury that curled her toes and made her eyes blaze and made her hair feel like it was standing up on end. Her bees' buzzing grew loud as a roar behind her words as she spoke them. "How dare you," she said, her voice shaking. "All of you." She pointed at Gnar and Lich and the rest of the Lords and Ladies. "This land and its people will never be ruled by anyone. And definitely"—she pointed straight at Arenthiel—"not by you."

She was bound to this land and its people, and she would show Arenthiel what that really meant. She waved her hand and her bees swarmed around her, buzzing furiously. She stamped her foot and the ground trembled. The deep-forest kin at the edge of the clearing swayed like trees in a growing wind. "How dare you come into my land, threatening my people," she shouted.

"We shall see about that, false Lady." Arenthiel gave a sharp gesture and his Lords and Ladies surged forward. Arrows flew; spears were lowered.

From all around her came snarls and shouts as her people responded, leaping to meet Arenthiel's hunt.

"Phouka!" she called, ducking an arrow that sizzled past just over her head. The horse kicked out with a forehoof, sending a Lady flying from the saddle of her goat-mount, and dashed across the clearing to her. "Watch Rook!" she shouted at the horse. "Don't let anybody hurt him."

Phouka snorted and, shouldering aside a charging Lord, trotted to the edge of the Way, where he stood over sleeping Rook, all four hooves planted, immovable.

In the clearing, arrows zipped past. A puck shifted in midleap, turning into a huge dog that carried a Lord off his mount and onto the ground. A clot of bees zoomed after a shrieking Lady. There were screams and shouts. The hunt's spears flashed in the sunlight.

Fer stepped farther into the clearing. "I've had just about enough of this," she murmured to herself. Under her feet she felt her land trembling. But not with fear. It was *waiting*. Waiting for her to call it forward, to join the fight.

"Lady, look out!" she heard Fray shout. Turning, she saw Arenthiel on his tall horse, charging toward her, drawing a long knife from his belt as he came.

She stood firm. The power in her land flowed up through her feet and legs, filling her whole body. She would *not* let them spill blood here.

The deep-forest kin were waiting; she could feel their roots trembling with anticipation. She nodded to them. *Now.* All over the clearing their roots exploded from the ground. Like whips they cracked through the air, sweeping Lords and Ladies off their mounts. She flicked a finger and grass grew up over the legs of their horses and goats and stags, bringing them to a snorting, wide-eyed standstill. More roots erupted from the dirt, looping themselves around Gnar and Lich, dragging them down to the ground.

A few Lords and Ladies squirmed out of the roots' hold and tried to flee; the deep-forest kin caught them in their branchlike arms, holding them more tightly the harder they fought to get away.

Silence fell. The bees returned to her, hovering over her head. Her own people and the pucks backed away from the root-imprisoned enemy.

Arenthiel pried himself up from the ground, kicking his feet free of the grass that caught at him, slashing at the roots with his knife. Her bees buzzed a warning as he paced toward her. His tawny beauty was smudged with dirt, but his eyes glittered golden and keen. "I have waited long enough for my time," he panted. "I am far more suited to rule this land than you are."

"Don't listen to him, Lady," shouted one of the pucks. The leader-puck, she thought it was. "He's rotten to the core—we can see it!"

"Curst pucks," Arenthiel hissed. "As soon as I am done with you, Gwynnefar, I will deal with them." Roots oozed up over his feet, and he kicked free of them and lurched toward her again.

She let him come, though she felt the land quivering, wanting to seize him. "I am the Lady of this land."

"You are a part-human interloper, and no Lady," he said, crouching, getting ready to spring.

"I know what I am," she said more quietly. She steadied herself and reached into the land.

As Arenthiel leaped toward her, raising the knife to strike, the ground opened under his feet. Down he sank, struggling wildly as tiny grass roots crawled over his skin and dirt surged up like a wave, until he was sunk into the ground up to his neck and covered with grass, all but his wide, golden eyes and his wide, gasping mouth. He struggled, but the land held him fast.

Fer went to crouch beside his head. Her anger evaporated, just like dew on a hot summer morning. She rested her fingers over where his ears were, and the grass pulled aside, so he could hear. "I know you stole the crown and that you planned to steal my land," she said calmly to his grass-covered face. "You've failed." She considered what she wanted to do with him. Not death. She couldn't stain the land with his blood. Hmm. "I think I want you to do two things," she said.

Arenthiel spat dirt from his mouth. His eyes narrowed. He started to hiss out a curse at her, and the grass crawled up over his face and snapped his mouth closed.

"Don't say anything," Fer said firmly.

The golden eyes glared at her. She pulled the seeing-stone out of her patch-jacket pocket and stared into his eyes, and now that she knew what to look for she could see past their beauty, deeper and deeper, and then she saw that the pucks were right—way down in there was something very, very old, akin to the High Ones, but also not like them at all, something using the shell of a beautiful body to do ugly, rotten things. The old thing in there resisted. She pushed back. This was a land of green, of long summer days, of fresh life. That rotten core didn't have any place here.

The resistance in his eyes shriveled.

Fer put the seeing-stone back into her jacket pocket. She tapped Arenthiel's mouth, and the grass let him catch a gasping breath. "I want you to swear to end the hunt and never hunt the pucks again," she said.

Silence. Then, in a cracked, ancient voice, he said, "I will never hunt again."

"Louder," Fer ordered.

He coughed out a clot of dirt. "I will never hunt again," he said. "Once, twice, three times I swear it."

"Thank you," Fer said, getting to her feet. She walked over the quivering ground to where Lich and Gnar were wrapped in roots and held by branches.

"Well, Strange One," Gnar said, still fiery, even with gnarled roots pinning her to the ground.

"She's a Lady," Lich gasped. One of the deep-forest kin held him in a tight embrace; he looked half squashed.

"Lady Strange One, then," Gnar said.

Fer sighed. She'd hoped maybe Lich and Gnar would be friends, but they weren't. "I'm not sure what to do with you," she told them.

"We know we shouldn't have listened to him." Gnar pointed with her sharp chin toward where Arenthiel's grassy head poked up out of the ground. "But we didn't know what you were up to."

She really was strange to them, Fer realized. She'd helped them once before, but helping, she realized, was not something they understood. Well then, they'd have to learn. "You are free," she told them. "The land will let you go if you'll swear to take off your glamories." She fixed them with something she hoped was a Ladylike glare. Then she spread the glare around, to include all the Lords and Ladies in the clearing. "You will *all* swear to take off your glamories. And you're all going to go back to your own lands and instead of ruling, you're going to figure out how to help the people who live there. Got it?"

"I swear it!" Gnar said, grinning. She ripped her arm loose of the ground and with her other hand started scrabbling at the sparkling web of glamorie that covered her. As it peeled off, the roots released her, and she staggered to her feet, shivering. She ripped off the last of the glamorie and dropped it to the grass. The ground opened where it landed and swallowed the glamorie up. Lich did the same, shivering as he tore the glamorie from his skin and dropped it to the ground.

The rest of the Lords and Ladies struggled free of their bindings and knelt on the grass. "We promise to remove the glamories," they swore, a binding oath. To break it would be to break their bonds with all the lands and their people. Several of them were weeping, and they were all pale and shaking.

"What about him?" Lich asked, pointing at Arenthiel's grass-covered head.

Right. Him. Fer went back and crouched beside him. "Two things, I said," she reminded him. "The second thing I want you to do is to go away from this land in peace. Will you swear to do that?"

"I swear it," he croaked, utterly defeated.

"Good." Fer waved her hand and the ground spat out Arenthiel; he landed in a dirty heap on the grass. He creaked to his feet. His golden skin sagged from his bones; his hair was caked with dirt, his eyes were dull. He looked around the clearing at the wreckage of his hunt; he looked down at himself and saw his perfection destroyed, and slowly, like a tree falling, he toppled over and lay facedown on the ground, unmoving.

Fer frowned. Was he injured? She went to him and pulled him over so she could see his face.

"Careful, Lady," Fray called.

"It's all right," Fer murmured. Arenthiel wasn't going to hurt her; not now. His skin had wrinkled and cracked; his eyes had sunken deep into his skull; even his hair had thinned and turned brittle.

Fer waved her hand, calling the bees. They hovered in front of her face. "Keep an eye on them," she said, and pointed at the Lords and Ladies. Then she turned to her own people. "Fray," she called.

The young wolf-guard stepped forward. "Yes, Fer-Lady!" she answered.

Fer grinned up at her; she grinned back. "I need some boiling water."

"Righty-o," Fray said.

Twig stepped up beside Fray and folded her arms just like the bigger wolf-guard. "What can I do, Lady?"

"I'll need rags for bandages too, and plenty of honey." Some of her people and the pucks had been injured in the brief battle—she had to get to work on them as soon as she could.

Her people leaped into action, racing to build fires and off to the Lady Tree for other supplies.

Fer reached into the pocket of her patch-jacket, pulling out the leather pouch that Rook had brought to her. She knew what she'd find inside. Herbs from Grand-Jane. There was lavender and valerian and mullein in labeled cloth bags. These were healing herbs; they were even more powerful on this side of the Way. She found a small jar of lavender honey, too, and an elderberry tincture, and there was even a little mortar and pestle wrapped in a cloth. It was exactly what she needed. Just like Grand-Jane, to think of everything.

With sure hands, Fer tipped herbs into the mortar. She looked up. More of her people and the Lords and Ladies gathered around; the pucks did too, keeping their distance. The leader-puck edged closer. "Our pup will be all right?" he asked. Rook, he meant.

Fer nodded. "I think so. You might find him some food for when he wakes up." He'd be ravenous when he did. Maybe they could find some rabbits to eat—that's what he liked. Now, she needed help with this. "You—" She pointed at the puck named Tatter.

"Me?" he asked, with a quick grin.

"I need you to grind up these herbs. Like this." She showed him the grinding motion, the one she'd learned by working for hours in Grand-Jane's stillroom. She handed him the mortar and pestle.

With a shrug, Tatter sat beside her and started to grind the herbs.

"You—" Fer pointed at Lich. "Run and tell Fray that we'll need plenty of blankets, too."

Lich bobbed his head and hurried away.

She took the top off the bottle of tincture and mixed some of it with the honey. "Is that all ground up?" she asked Tatter.

"It is, yes," he said.

She took the mortar from him and set it on the ground. Fray came up with a clay pot full of boiling water. "Good," Fer said, taking it from her. She put the ground herbs into the hot water, then added the honey and tincture.

She lifted Arenthiel's head and held the cup to his dry lips. The healing tea dribbled down his chin. "Tatter," she said. "I need you to hold him up."

As the Lords and Ladies stared, Tatter knelt beside Arenthiel and gently eased him up so Fer could feed him the medicine. But his eyes stayed closed and more tea was wasted. Fer let out a frustrated sigh. She wanted to help him, but this wasn't working.

"You're not doing it right," Tatter said.

"Oh, really," Fer muttered, trying again. "Who's the healer here, me or you?"

The puck laughed. "I'll be needing a bit of cloth," he said.

Okay, fine. Setting down the tea, Fer ripped a patch from her jacket and handed it to him.

"This'll do very well," Tatter said. He dipped a corner of the patch into the tea. Then he gently pried open

Arenthiel's mouth and put in a fold of the wet cloth. He did this over and over again, patiently feeding Arenthiel the medicine, while the Lords and Ladies watched.

Finally Arenthiel gave a weak cough, and his eyes opened. With steady hands, Tatter took the cup of medicine and fed it to him, sip after sip. When the cup was empty, he handed it to Fer with a sharp grin. "It's all right, Fer-Lady. He'll do."

twenty-five

After tending to everyone who'd been injured in the fight—both her own people and the Lords and Ladies— and setting the badger-men to looking after all the mounts, and thanking the deep-forest kin before they left to return to the thickly wooded valley they lived in, Fer got ready to take Arenthiel back to the nathe. The High Ones would have to decide what to do with him.

As they stood under the Lady Tree, Fray and Twig tried to convince her to stay. "Your place is here, Lady, not in that nasty nathe," Fray said. Beside her, Twig nodded.

"Don't worry," Fer reassured them. "I'll go quickly and come right back home. I need you to stay here and keep an eye on things." She nodded toward the edge of the forest where the pucks lurked in a shadowy group, Rook still asleep in their midst, then at the one Lord and two Ladies who were too injured to travel with the rest of them. She didn't think there'd be trouble, but she needed Fray and Twig here, just in case.

Tatter came up, leading Arenthiel's horse. Arenthiel himself sat slumped on its back, wrapped in a blanket. "He's all ready to go," the puck said. "Tell the High Ones that we pucks have given him a new name." He leaned over and whispered in her ear.

"Tatter!" Fer said, half laughing. "That's an awful name!"

"You tell them," Tatter said, still grinning. "If they don't call him by his proper puck name, we'll be hearing about it, and then there'll be terrible trouble for them."

She bet there would. "Okay, I'll tell them," she promised.

"And there's this," Tatter said. He handed her a bag. "It was tied to the back of his horse's saddle." Arenthiel's, he meant.

Fer opened the bag. Inside, wrapped in midnight-blue velvet, was the silver crown. Good. The High Ones had said in front of everyone that the one who returned the crown would win the competition. They wouldn't have any choice but to confirm that she was the Lady of the Summerlands.

Tatter handed her the reins of Arenthiel's horse, and she said good-bye and walked along the path through the forest. Her bees buzzed lazily over her head, contented in the golden light of the setting sun. The late afternoon was full of rustling leaves and the humming of her bees. In the distance, she could hear a stream rushing over rocks. She followed the path until she reached the Way that would take her to the Lake of All Ways and the nathe. The Lords and Ladies and Gnar and Lich were waiting. Phouka was waiting too.

Fer handed the reins of Arenthiel's horse to Lich and went over to Phouka. "Are you coming?" she asked.

He leaned his head forward and whuffled into her neck. It tickled.

She grabbed his mane and swung up onto his back, careful not to drop the bag with the crown in it, then waited with the Lords and Ladies for the sun to go down. As the day turned to night, she led them into the Way they'd battered through—something she'd have to fix later, she reminded herself. Arenthiel came last, silent and huddled in his blanket.

They came out on the bank of the Lake of All Ways and the High Ones were waiting for them with the rest of the nathe, standing before the vine-wall with the half-moon rising behind them.

Fer climbed down from Phouka's back, feeling

suddenly very small and grubby. And tired, too. She took a deep, steadying breath. She hadn't lost her leafy crown; that was something. It was still as fresh and green as ever on top of her head. And she had the bag with the silver crown in it.

As always, Lord Artos, the bear-man, stepped up to speak for the High Ones. "Explain yourself, Gwynnefar," he said sternly.

"*Lady* Gwynnefar," Fer corrected.

She opened the bag and pulled out the velvet-wrapped package inside. Unwrapping it, she laid the silver crown at the High Ones' feet. In the moonlight, it shone with gentle radiance. But its beauty couldn't trick her. "That's the crown you offered," she said. "But I don't want it. I like my own crown better." She reached up to touch the circlet of leaves and twigs. Then she told them everything, that Arenthiel had stolen the crown and framed Rook for it, that he'd tried to cheat in the contest to win the Lordship of the Summerlands. And that he'd failed. "You should find something for him to do," she said, pointing at Arenthiel, "besides plotting."

And she had another thing to say to the High Ones.

"You, and all the rest of you—" She pointed at all the Lords and Ladies of the nathe who had gathered in the chilly moonlight. "You've got it the wrong way around. Sometimes some people have more power than others.

It's that way in the human world too. But those with power should do good things with it. If you are true Lords and Ladies, you won't command them with your glamories; you won't demand that your people swear oaths to you. You should swear to serve them, and to serve your lands."

She finished. Maybe they would listen to her, and maybe they wouldn't. "I *am* the Lady of the Summerlands," she added, just to be sure they understood. "I am sworn to serve all my people."

There was a moment of shocked silence, and then the High Ones glided forward, stepping past the silver crown, as graceful as birch trees swaying in the wind. Their power washed over Fer. It was stronger than any glamorie, ancient and—somehow—pure. Fer closed her eyes, feeling how deeply the High Ones belonged here, in this place.

Lord Artos opened his mouth to speak for them, but then one of the High Ones waved him silent and beckoned to Fer.

On shaky legs, Fer went over to stand before them. She knew she was supposed to bow her head and kneel, but she steadied herself and stayed on her feet. She looked up at the High Ones.

Their eyes were ancient and deep and knowing. "Did you know, Gwynnefar," one of them said in her flowing-water voice, "that you nearly lost the competition in the final round?"

Fer took a deep breath. "Because I took off the glamorie?"

"No," the High One said. Her voice was smiling, even though her dappled face stayed still and smooth. "Because you put it on."

"Ohhh." Fer breathed. It really *had* been a test.

"Your mother . . ." one of the High Ones began.

"Your mother, the Lady Laurelin," the other continued, "refused to wear the glamorie. She was the first Lady ever to do so." Ignoring Fer's gasp of surprise, the High One went on. "It was a terrible risk she took. Because she did not rule her people as a Lady should, one of her people—the crow-warrior, the Mór—rebelled against the oath she had sworn your mother. The Mór took the glamorie for herself; she killed your mother and attempted to rule as Lady in her place."

"Thanks to you, Gwynnefar," the first High One put in, "she failed."

"But we wonder . . ." the other High One began.

"Yes, we wonder," the first continued smoothly. "Was your mother right to refuse to rule?"

There was a cool silence. When Fer spoke, she felt like her words were dropping like stones into still water, spreading ripples as they fell. "My mother was right," she said steadily. "To rule is wrong."

The Lords and Ladies gathered behind the High Ones stirred at that, and murmured to one another.

"Arenthiel was right about one thing," a High One said. "You are dangerous, Fer. As your mother was before you. Time passes slowly here, and in some places, not at all. Change does not come often to these lands. You bring change." She paused, and Fer saw a flash of something in her dark eyes, like a ripple passing over deepest water. "Whether that change is for good or for evil, we have yet to discover."

There was a long, still silence.

"I—I think it's good," Fer said. She hoped it was.

"See that it is so," the High One said.

Trembling, Fer nodded. "I will." The High One nodded. Fer was dismissed, she understood. Trying not to stumble with sudden weariness, Fer crossed the grass and climbed onto Phouka's back. Time to go home.

Oops, she'd almost forgotten. "The pucks helped save Arenthiel's life," she said to the High Ones. "And they gave him a new name. Will you make sure he's called by that name from now on?"

"We will, Lady Gwynnefar," the High One answered, all solemn and beautiful under the silver moonlight.

Fer felt a sudden lightness in her heart. She grinned down at them from Phouka's back. "The pucks named him Old Scrawny. They'll know if you change it, so that's what you'd better call him."

The High Ones nodded at that. Then they used their power to open the Way for her. Leaving Old Scrawny to his fate, Fer rode through the opened Way, going back to her own land—to her home, and to her kin.

* * *

When Rook woke up under Fer's Lady Tree, it was night and his puck-brother Asher was kneeling on the ground next to him, building a fire. Tatter sat on a thick root, and Rip crouched in the shadows nearby.

"Where's Fer?" Rook asked, pushing the blankets off and sitting up. How long had he been asleep? What had happened with Arenthiel's hunt? Things must have worked out all right, or his brothers wouldn't be here. He stretched. His stomach felt like a gaping black cavernous cave of emptiness. "Ow. Is there anything to eat?"

"There will be in a moment, Pup," Asher answered, and tossed more wood onto the fire, then held a spitted rabbit over the flames.

"You don't have to cook it too much," Rook said, leaning forward. "I don't mind it a little bloody."

Asher laughed at him.

Rook stared at the rabbit, watching juices drip into the fire as it cooked. His mouth watered. His stomach was going to eat *him* if he didn't put something in it soon.

"You asked about the Lady," Rip growled from the shadows. "Before you asked about your brothers."

Whoops. "They're all well?" Rook asked. "Is that done yet?" he said to Asher.

"Not yet, Pup," his brother-puck answered with a grin. "And yes, we're all well. Thanks to that Lady of yours."

Rip moved out of the shadows. He was hard to see in the firelight, with his red-and-black-painted skin. "Are you bound to the Fer-Lady, Rook?" he asked, his teeth gleaming.

"It seems like you are," Tatter put in from his log.

Rook blinked. He was. Sort of. The thread he'd felt before, the one he'd broken twice, had spun itself out again, connecting him to Fer. It was just a cobweb of a thread; he could easily break it again. That would make three times, and the thread would never connect them again.

"It's her binding magic," Rip growled.

Rook shook his head. "I've been bound before, to the Mór, and this is nothing like that." He nodded at the fire. "I think that's done, Asher."

His brother-puck pulled the rabbit off the fire. "It's not binding magic she's using, but it's something," Asher said slowly. He handed the cooked rabbit to Rook. "Careful, it's hot."

Ignoring his brother-puck's warning, Rook ripped into the rabbit. Mmmm, perfectly bloody, just as he liked it. Juices ran down his chin and he tore off a leg, gnawing it down to the bone.

"Something," Tatter put in. "That Lady of yours has something about her. I can feel it too."

"Doesn't matter," Rip said. "We're not bound to her."

"She offered us safety here," Tatter argued. He leaned forward, and his yellow eyes reflected the firelight. "She's our back way out, our safe place. There aren't any oaths between us, but she's our Lady, whether we like it or not."

"Not," said Rip fiercely. "We are *pucks*. She is not our Lady."

"Maybe you're right." Tatter shrugged. "It's clear, anyway, that she doesn't understand what a puck truly is."

Rip gave a nasty grin. "We'll show her, then, won't we."

"Well, we're not tame, at any rate," Asher said, getting to his feet. "The other lands are safer for us now. We'll be leaving when the moon gets a little higher; we'll wait at the Way and go through as soon as the sun rises and it opens." He gazed down at Rook. "You can come with us, Pup, as you please. We'll be glad if you do, and we'll be back in this land again to see you if you don't. You choose."

Asher faded into the shadows. Rip followed. Tatter shot him a quick grin and then left too.

Rook put down the rabbit and got to his feet, ready to follow them. They were his brothers; he needed to follow. But the thread of connection still tied him to Fer. All he had to do was break it, and then he would go.

* * *

Fer came through the Way from the nathe, landing in the dark clearing. Phouka was tired too. He trotted along the path to his favorite meadow, where he stopped. She yawned as she slid off his broad back. The meadow smelled of grass warmed by the sun all day, and clover, and of the falling dew. "Thanks for the ride," she whispered to Phouka, and leaned against his warm, solid side. She felt tired down to her bones. Maybe she could just lie down in the meadow and sleep until morning.

Phouka snorted.

"I know." She straightened and patted him once more on the neck, then headed for the Lady Tree. The summer night felt cool and soft; stars twinkled overhead and a fingernail moon crept up over the trees.

A dark shadow loomed on the path before her, and before she could even catch her breath she was surrounded by pucks who jostled past her, bumping her off the path, their eyes flaming in the night. "Farewell, Lady," one of them said; she heard a laugh and caught a glimpse of sharp teeth. Then they faded into the night and were gone.

She stared after them. The pucks, leaving. Had Rook gone with them? He might have—she'd seen a familiar-looking dog in their midst. If he was awake and well enough, he must have gone. With a sad sigh, she turned back to the path and headed on toward the Lady Tree.

As she came nearer, she saw that the lights of the houses in its branches were out; her people were asleep.

No, not everybody was asleep, she realized. There was an orange glow coming from the other side of the Lady Tree. She padded through the grass and came around the Tree and stopped, staring.

Sitting around a campfire were Fray and Twig, each with a cup of tea in her hands. Circling the fire, Fer sat down next to them. In the tree overhead, she heard her bees buzzing sleepily.

"Hello, Fer-Lady," Fray said.

"Hello," Twig echoed, and then gave a huge yawn. She leaned her head against Fray's broad shoulder and sighed.

"Everything's okay?" Fer asked.

"Yup," Fray said. "All well."

"Is there any more tea?"

Fray nodded and reached for the kettle that was keeping warm next to the fire.

"It's all right, I'll get it," Fer said. She didn't want to disturb Twig, who was now fast asleep. Quietly she found a cup and poured out tea.

"We thought maybe the High Ones would try to make you stay at the nathe," Fray said.

"Oh no," Fer answered, and yawned. "I wanted to come home." She settled with her back against the Lady Tree, feeling its solid strength, its branches reaching high up into the starry sky, its roots plunging down into the darkest depths of the ground. All was well in her land. It would be even better if Rook were here, but she knew him well enough. He'd be back, and she could figure out then if they were really friends or not. She took a sip of tea and sighed with perfect happiness.

"That was a strange thing you did, Fer-Lady," Fray said. "Swearing your oath to us." She was silent for a moment, as if thinking. "It feels different."

"It is different." Fer remembered what the High Ones had said. "It's a change."

"What does it mean?" Fray persisted.

Fer gave her a sleepy smile. "It means we are friends, Fray."

The wolf-girl nodded, smiling back. "Friends, yes, Lady. And we are kin, too."

Yes. And kin, too.

Acknowledgments

Many thanks . . .

To this book's intrepid first readers: Greg van Eekhout, Deb Coates, Rae Carson, and Jenn Reese.

To my editor, Antonia Markiet, whose wise guidance helped me unravel this book and knit it back together again.

To my agent, Caitlin Blasdell, whose critiques always make me a stronger writer. Thanks, too, to the Liza Dawson Agency.

To the wonderful HarperCollins team, starting with associate editor Rachel Abrams, and then editor Alyson Day, senior production editor Kathryn Silsand, editorial director Phoebe Yeh, president and publisher Susan Katz, senior art director Amy Ryan, senior designer Tom

Forget, production director Lucille Schneider, associate publicist Olivia DeLeon, and cover artist Jason Chan.

To Connie Mutel, whose book *The Emerald Horizon: The History of Nature in Iowa* has shaped my understanding of what it means for land to be tame, and for it to be wild.

To Dozer van Eekhout-Will of the flopped-over ear.

Jon Michael Hansen for archery, Jennifer Adam for horsery, Deb Coates for doggery.

To my parents, my grrrl-power sisters—Kate, Maude, and Winnie—and to my husband and wildling children.

Ingrid, is it time for lunch?